Food Fight

Published in the United States in 2019
Published in Canada by Fitzhenry & Whiteside

195 Allstate Parkway, Markham, ON L3R 4T8
Published in the United States by Fitzhenry & Whiteside
311 Washington Street, Brighton, MA 02135

2 4 6 8 10 9 7 5 3 1

Library and Archives Canada Cataloguing in Publication

Sherman, Deborah (Deborah Faye), author
Food fight / Deborah Sherman.

ISBN 978-1-55455-391-4 (softcover)

I. Title.

PS8637.H487F66 2018   jC813'.6   C2018-905069-1

Publisher Cataloging-in-Publication Data (U.S.)

Names: Sherman, Deborah (Deborah Faye), author.
Title: Food Fight / Deborah Sherman.
Description: Markham, Ontario : Fitzhenry & Whiteside, 2018. | Summary: "Personal rivalries,
emotions, ambitions, friendships, politics and competition converge during a high school election
campaign in this fast-paced fun-filled character-driven story" – Provided by publisher.
Identifiers: ISBN 978-1-55455-391-4 (paperback)
Subjects: LCSH: Elections –Juvenile fiction. | Competition – Juvenile fiction. | High school students
– Juvenile fiction. | BISAC: JUVENILE FICTION / Social Themes / Friendship.
Classification: LCC PZ7.S547Fo | DDC 813.6 – dc23

Design by Tanya Montini
Printed in Canada by Copywell

Fitzhenry & Whiteside acknowledges with thanks the Canada Council for the Arts
and the Ontario Arts Council for their support of our publishing program.

We acknowledge the financial support of the Government of Canada through
the Canada Book Fund (CBF) for our publishing activities.

www.fitzhenry.ca

Food Fight

DEBORAH SHERMAN

Fitzhenry & Whiteside

The Crime Scene

There was no doubt about it. It was the potatoes' fault.

Plopping off the ceiling in goopy chunks. (It wasn't mashed well this morning.) Oozing off the table and onto the floor in a big lumpy mess. (Some of the lumps were the size of golf balls!) Coating notebooks, textbooks, pens, pencils, erasers and knapsacks in white, gloppy sludge.

There was no doubt about it: the mushy mashed potatoes made things look bad. Very bad. Green beans had been tossed around too, but they didn't stick to the tables and chairs. Meatloaf had also been chucked around. But meatloaf didn't slowly inch its way down the cafeteria walls. That was the potato. The meatloaf hit the wall and fell quickly to the floor—though it did leave behind a grim copper-brown stain.

Everyone in the cafeteria stood in a stunned silence. It was so quiet that one could hear a pin drop—or, in this case, a green bean *plonk* to the floor. The eerie stillness made it hard to believe that just moments ago kids were hooting and hollering and ducking for cover as vegetables flew through the air at high speed. Most of the J.R. Wilcott student body was covered in a rainbow-coloured sludge. Laundry would have to be done tonight with extra-strength detergent. One or two students still had fists full of veggies cocked, ready to let loose.

Yes, it was bad. The worst food fight in J.R. Wilcott's history. Beans, meatloaf, orange juice and apple pie all littered the floor. But, worst of all was the big glop of mashed potato covering J.R. Wilcott's math teacher, Mr. Papernick. Never in a good mood on the best of days, Mr. Papernick angrily wiped potatoes from his brow. His anger turned to fury when he noticed the stack of papers in his hands. They were completely destroyed by the flying spuds!

The three suspects were already being marched to Principal Losman's office. They left a guilty trail of smushy footprints behind them. Someone was going to pay— and heavily. Detention if he or she were lucky; suspension if the principal was in a bad mood; expulsion if an example was to be set. Yes, once this whole mess was sorted out, someone would be in big trouble. It might have been the mashed potato's fault, but vegetables can't serve detention.

Chapter One

SUSPECT NUMBER ONE

☞ Andrea Hackenpack

Some of it might have been my fault. Okay, so 30 to 35 percent of it might have been my fault. But indirectly. Not on purpose! A giant food fight was not part of the plan. In fact, it was pretty opposite to the plan. I've always believed that it's important to be noticed and discussed—to make yourself unforgettable. But this was not the kind of notice I was after. If I were more tech-savvy, this never would have happened.

I've had a master plan for myself ever since Kindergarten: scholarship to Fitzpatrick All-Girls Private High School, Harvard undergrad, Yale Law School, an internship with the Governor General and then a job in Parliament. Grades are important. I carry an A minus average. (Gym has always been a hurdle—no pun intended—for me.) But, extra-curricular activities are the key to getting into a good private school. All of the girls applying to Fitzpatrick have top grades. It's what you do outside of the classroom that counts.

"I'm hoping my extra-curriculars are a reflection of my personality," I told my guidance counselor, Ms. Buhari, at the beginning of the year. We meet once a month, at my request, to make sure I'm on the right track. "I hope to be like a good ice cream."

"Complex but satisfying," I said trying to erase the look of confusion on her face. "Serious and trustworthy with a ribbon of fun running through."

"If you say so, Andrea," she replied, still looking confused.

Currently, I play percussion in the school band (after an unhappy stint with a guitar) and serve my J.R. Wilcott community as student council secretary. The notes I record during our meetings are legendary for their length and detail. The other kids love them because they ensure we miss a whole period of algebra. I just want to make sure I leave no detail, no matter how big or small, out.

But my extra-curricular activities don't end there. I swim freestyle on the swim team and, up until last month, I was the editor of the Grade Seven Gazette, a monthly newspaper. At our last meeting, Mr. Kagan, my English teacher, informed me that our readership was pretty much non-existent and shut down the paper.

"Please reconsider," I begged him. "The competition to get into Fitzpatrick All-Girls Private High School is massive. I need as many activities on my resume as possible!"

"The paper's a bit dry, Andrea. I'm not sure if your peers are interested in your coverage of this year's District Principal Summit at McKelvin Junior High. You need to come up with ways to spice the paper up. Maybe an advice column or perhaps horoscopes? Then we can talk about starting it up again—maybe online this time so we can save costs."

The closure of the paper was a blow but it didn't deter me from the next, and most vital, stage in my plan: becoming student body president of J.R. Wilcott. The presidency has always been a sure-fire way to make your mark at school—a way to get yourself noticed and discussed. Our outgoing president, Michael Wise, is probably the most popular president in J.R. Wilcott history. Highlights of his legacy include getting pizza served for lunch three times a week and pulling off an amazing school play. He is a legend around the hallowed halls of Wilcott.

Elections were less than a month away and I was up against some major competition. Marty Jenkins was a frontrunner. He had just revealed himself to be a champion competitive eater and was reveling in the glory of his newfound popularity. I had known Marty since our early days in Kindergarten when we battled fiercely over who would be picked to feed the class goldfish. He lost and was stuck being coat monitor instead. I'm not sure he ever got over it. Gwenn Yoon was my other competition. She had already spent time on student council and was shy but well liked. And Sludge Sludinksy, the lead in this year's school play, was debating running.

"But you're already in grade eight," I reminded him. "You won't be here next year."

"I will if I can't get my math grade up," he replied frowning. Sludge was one of the most popular guys at J.R Wilcott. I thought about offering to tutor him.

With or without Sludge, the competition would be stiff. I knew I had to do something spectacular if I wanted to get elected. In some ways, this whole mess is Mr. Kagan's fault. He was the one who put the idea of an advice column in my head. If only I hadn't spent so much time researching the last thirty years of historical rulings at the District Principal Summit and a little more time on IT. I'm just hoping this little blip on my record doesn't spoil my master plan. It would be a shame if a smidgen of mashed potato ruined my chances to go to Fitzpatrick All-Girls Private High School.

Chapter Two

SUSPECT NUMBER TWO
☞ Ralph Dorph

All I wanted to do was make a few friends. One or two good friends.

"Not again!" I complained when my parents told me we were moving. "This will be my fifth school in six years."

"I know it's hard but we have to go where the work is," said my mother sympathetically.

My dad's a geologist and while it's been fun to live in places like Japan and France, it's really tough to be on the move all the time.

"You'll make friends in no time, champ," said my father cheerfully. "You always do."

I nodded silently and dropped the subject. Neither of my parents understood what it was like to go to a new school. They tried to make it easier on me. This time, they got me an iPhone so I wasn't completely on my own.

"Call us during lunch time so we can hear how it's going," said my mom.

But they never had to walk into a classroom and have thirty pairs of eyes sizing them up with most of those eyes quickly deciding I had transferred from Dorkville Junior High. Each school had a different set of rules and by the time I had finally figured them out, my parents announced we were moving on.

"Cool to be on the chess club at Dover Middle School," I reported to my big sister, Mara.

"Not cool to be on the chess club at Nelson Prep," I reported a few months later.

"Plaid turtlenecks and corduroys not cool anywhere, Ralphie," she replied eyeing my wardrobe. "Maybe you'll get lucky this time and at J.R. Wilcott it will be cool to be totally uncool."

"Yeah, hopefully my complete lack of a lay-up, feeble wrist-shot and noodle arm will make me a superstar," I said laughing nervously.

Mara slung a sympathetic arm over my shoulder. "Just try and take advantage of any opportunities that come your way, Ralphie, and you'll find a way to make friends."

At the time, I wasn't sure what she meant. But, when I saw

the advertisement on the J.R. Wilcott notice board I suddenly knew exactly what Mara meant! I had no idea that a month later I would be accused of starting a gigantic food fight and would be making my way to the principal's office.

Chapter Three

SUSPECT NUMBER THREE
☞ Joe Jacobs

I love a good food fight! Usually it's around the dinner table and starts when one of my brothers asks me to pass a slice of bread. It usually ends when my mother sends me to my room.

With two older bros, I have tons of experience with food fights. Sliced bread doesn't shoot through the air so well but I can sling a dinner roll clear across the room, no sweat. Brussel sprouts are gross to eat but great to throw. Cauliflower is surprisingly awesome to hurl; broccoli not so much. My mom got so sick of food flying around the dinner table that she started a no chucking chow policy. First offenders get booted from the table. Repeat offenders are punished by no TV for the night.

"Coach said I need to work on my fastball," I tried last week after firing a peach at my brother, Marcus.

"Lighten up, Ma. At least it wasn't a grapefruit this time," said Marcus in my defence. He licked the peach juice trickling down his arm. "Juicy!"

She didn't buy it for a second and I missed watching the whole hockey game—playoff hockey! My oldest brother, Mario, was cool enough to smuggle me his phone so I could get scoring updates on his hockey app. My mom's tough. The Jacobs bro who starts the food fight gets an extra two TV-less nights. We have to read instead— and no sports sections allowed. A real book!

Mashed potatoes are not on my shortlist of awesome things to pelt people with. Baked potatoes are a much better choice. Double the distance with half the effort—though they can result in a nasty stinger if they're undercooked. I have a sixth sense when it comes to projectile potatoes.

I didn't have a fighting chance once I saw the flying taters.

Chapter Four

SUSPECT NUMBER ONE
☞ Andrea Hackenpack

"I need to do something to make my mark on this school—to make people really see how much good I can accomplish if I'm elected president. Rumour has it Marty Jenkins is offering competitive eating lessons for anyone who votes for him. Four meatball hoagies in four minutes—minus water to wash them down. How can I top that?"

"Hmm. Yup. Sure. Uh huh, Andrea." My best friend, Jenny Mitchell, was looking at her iPhone. She nodded periodically but her eyes never left the screen in front of her.

I had already wallpapered the school in posters, thematically announcing my candidacy. I still stand by my theme, *Andrea Hackenpack—Better than Ice Cream*. I thought it both showed off my fun side and got right down to business. Each poster was colour-coded and corresponded with a value I stood for. My mint (chocolate chip) posters detailed my plan on having the cafeteria go fully organic. My strawberry-coloured posters explained my idea of having free sunscreen available in all school bathrooms so no one would get a sunburn when they went outside for recess. My dark brown posters were specifically designed to show off my light-hearted nature—requesting chocolate ice cream (and sauce, of course) for all on Fridays. But any attention the posters gathered had melted fast. Letters of reference from my fellow student council colleagues were also quickly forgotten.

"Our futures are right around the corner, Jenny!" I said trying to get her full attention. "If you want to be vice-prez to my prez next year we're really going to have to step it up. Marty's campaign *Eating Your Way to the Top* will be hard to beat."

She nodded again but continued to read.

Exasperated, I grabbed her phone and quickly glanced down to see an avatar that looked a lot like Jenny but more colourful. "This is more important than discussing our futures?"

She snatched it back. "It's a new app that let's you combine different clothes and shows how you'd look in them. If you click and hold, it says where you can find the stuff you like. My mom won't let me wear heels to school but I'm pretty sure I can convince her to let me do a mini-wedge."

"Since when do you find your clothes on apps?" I asked, briefly forgetting my agenda. "You love the mall. If I can't find you at home, I just head to the second floor of Mapleville Mall."

"My brother just gave me his old phone and it's got a ton of space on it. I'm seeing what apps I can download for free. This one's awesome. It'll lead me right to a fabulous new wardrobe. Summer's almost here and I want to look good!" She looked me up and down. "You should think about downloading it, too, Andrea. Image is half the battle."

"Duly noted, Jen, but now's not the time for shirt and shoe apps," I said trying to hide my frustration at the change of subject. "Being vice president would be a pretty deal on your high school application, too. I know your parents are still upset that you quit band. This could be something that could get you back in their good books. I bet they'd start driving you to the mall again, right? Put your phone down and help me. I need an idea that will help me reach different pockets of Wilcotters and not just the Sevens I share classes with."

"You need a relaxation app," said Jenny laughing. "Take some of my advice for once. Chill and stop being a know-it-all trying to run everyone's life. Things will work out. Especially if I have these new wedges on my feet by next week. According to this I can find them at—"

But I was no longer listening to what Jenny was saying. I

was stuck on what she had *just* said. "You think I'm a know-it-all?" I asked her.

Jenny waited a moment before answering. She took a long sip of her drink. "Pretty much," she finally said. Jenny looked confused. She had just insulted me but I was smiling. She was on to something!

"A total-control-freak. A super bossypants," Jenny said, picking up on my new mood. She looked happy to be discussing a new subject. "You stick your nose in everyone's business and try to solve everyone's problems. Even people you don't know. Remember that guy in our sailing class last year? He couldn't tie a knot and you insisted on giving him extra practice. I wonder if he ever made it to shore? I hope he had a paddle in that boat because it wasn't very windy and he drifted pretty far out—"

Suddenly I knew how to make my mark at J.R.Wilcott. I would create an online advice column for my fellow Wilcotters. An advice app! My fellow students could tell me their problems and I would solve them with my words of wisdom. According to Jenny (and everyone in my family and my teachers and my sailing instructor) bossing people around was something I had a talent for. It was time I put this talent to official use!

Last impressions are just as important as first ones; I wanted Wilcotters to head to the voting booth with me on their minds.

It was vital that I end my campaign with a bang. And this would be it: a surprise that would blow everyone out of the water!

My advice app would be completely anonymous from both ends. No one would know it was me. In the upcoming weeks, my advice-giving talents would drastically improve the lives of all my fellow Wilcotters. Even though the advice would be anonymous, I would post testimonials from satisfied customers and even a few re-enactments of my customers' successes. I would amass a huge online following that reached all corners of Wilcott! Then, right before elections, I would reveal myself as Wilcott's own *Ms. Fix-it*. Wilcotters would head to the voting booth with clear evidence that I was true leadership material. This would easily outclass Marty's lame cuisine campaign. I just needed to find someone who could help me create the app. How hard could that be?

App created and ready to download? Check!

Creating my Bossypants app (™!) turned out to be simple. I scoped out the AV club in an effort to find Wilcott's biggest techie. It wasn't a surprise that my sights landed on Harold Wormald. Every fall he returned to school with impossibly thicker glasses than the year before. His eyes resembled mini-marbles hiding behind a giant wall of glass. They revealed just how much time he spent staring at a computer screen. Both his index fingers sported blisters.

"Too much time on the Wii this weekend. It broke just as I was on my way to bowling a perfect game. Had to open up the machine and fix it myself—and then finish my perfect game," he bragged, confirming my suspicions that I had found the right man for the job.

"How do you feel about doing me a little favour?" I asked him tentatively. I had my doubts if Harold did favours for people. His marble eyes narrowed slightly behind the thick pane of glass.

"Favour?" He repeated the word as if it was the first time ever hearing it.

My suspicions were on target. I quickly changed tactics. "I'll pay you twenty dollars if you can help me create an app." Now I was speaking a language he understood.

"I'm all ears," he said grabbing a pen from his pocket protector and whipping out a pad of paper from his sleeve.

Harold made notes as I explained my idea to him. He nodded periodically as I told him what functions I needed. "Easy-to-use interface. Anonymity. Quick turnaround. Should be pretty simple to create. I'm glad you came to me, Andrea," he said confidently.

A rush of energy shot through me and I broke out in a huge grin. "Excellent!"

"It's pretty nice of you to offer Wilcott free advice," he added as he smiled in return.

Though I had gone to school with Harold for years, I didn't know him very well. He was a year older than me. But, he was turning out to be friendlier than I'd expected. There was something about his smile that made me open up to him.

"Well, Jenny—Mitchell, my best friend—has been calling me a know-it-all forever. I realized I could put that *skill* to good use; I really need to utilize my strengths if I'm going to win the school presidency. Marty Jenkins is tough competition. People seem to love his ability to eat 101 meatballs in less than—"

"Jenkins has grand plans, too?" Harold inquired cutting me off.

I nodded. "I'm bracing myself for some tough competition. I need to have all my ducks in order and be ready to execute my plan with pinpoint precision. You must understand where I'm coming from." Harold had run his own—albeit losing—presidential campaign last year.

"Been there, done that, Hackenpack. I'm in the eighth grade now. Next year I'll be dealing with the real world—high school," he sniffed superiorly. This was the Harold I had expected. His tone softened. "But I really think your app is a great idea. Give me a few days and I'll have something to deliver."

"Thanks, Harold." I stuck out my hand and we shook on our deal.

Chapter Five

SUSPECT NUMBER TWO
☞ Ralph Dorph

It was the colour of the paper that first caught my eye. Bright pink. Not my favourite colour but effective.

I had been at J.R. Wilcott for over a week but yet to make solid contact with anyone. Sure, kids smiled when Mr. Kagan introduced me in English class and some gangly guy bouncing a basketball had given me a friendly punch in the arm, but I was eating my lunch alone. The chess club was meeting soon so I knew I'd have the chance to meet a few kids but, still, I was feeling lonely. I'd been on the chess club at Fujita International School, L'Ecole du Paris Nord and Shaker Heights Middle School so I knew what to expect—rooks, knights and bishops. Even though I was good at chess, I didn't love playing the game. In fact, I barely liked it.

"Same old, same old," I complained to Mara.

"Then put yourself out there. New school. New experiences," she replied trying to do the splits. She had decided to try out for her high school's musical even though she couldn't sing or dance. "Think of this as a chance to re-create yourself. No one at Wilcott knows about your nerd tendencies—though the plaid turtlenecks are a bit of a give-away. Put on a plain t-shirt and you can be a whole new Ralphie." She plonked a baseball cap on my head and laughed. "Ralph Dorph hitting clean up today!"

"I'm not exactly sporty," I complained. "I'll never make the basketball or volleyball team. Skateboarding isn't going to happen because I have weak ankles. And the swim team is out because chlorine makes me break out in hives. Ugh. Why did we have to move here? I was just starting to get comfortable at the last school." I knew I sounded whiny but I couldn't help myself.

Mara gave me a hug. "Sometimes it takes a little longer with the quiet ones, but don't worry so much. You'll find a way to fit in."

The bright pink flyer seemed to offer just that: a way to fit in. Maybe it was cheating—too much of a short-cut. Perhaps I should have listened to my sister and been patient. Maybe that's why it all backfired. But I was tired of eating my lunch alone.

Chapter Six

SUSPECT NUMBER THREE
☞ Joe Jacobs

I did it because of a girl. I saw the hot pink advertisement and just knew it was her. I had my eye on Daniela Olafson for a while. I knew I'd get chirped by the guys because she was younger than me but, man, she had awesome hair—long and fire-engine red. It was the same colour as my baseball jersey. Normally I don't stop and read things—especially if they are on the school bulletin board—but that paper was so bright. I stopped dribbling my ball and checked it out.

Attention J.R. Wilcott!!!

Are you secretly crushing on that girl

in chemistry class?

Dreaming of the hottie at the pencil

sharpener but don't know how to tell him?

Not sure how to get Mr. Kagan to give you an
extension on your book report?
Puzzled why you're not popular? Pulled in too
many directions because you're too popular?
Trying to convince your parents to stop
putting notes in your lunch box?
Whatever the problem, Dear Bossypants
(™!) can help you! Download the
Bossypants app and get all the free advice
you need! Complete anonymity is assured
when you write to Dear Bossypants. And
helpful, life-changing, brilliant words of
wisdom are guaranteed within 24 hours.
Download the app now for amazing advice!

My gut, plus a bit of simple logic, told me Daniela was behind this. Daniela starts with *D* and so does *Dear*. The second letter in Daniela's name is *a*; the third letter in Dear Bossypants is *a*. The name Bossypants was the most obvious giveaway: from what I can see, Daniela is often bossy and she usually wears pants to school. It was pretty obvious Daniela Olafson was behind the Dear Bossypants app!

Normally, I would go to one of my bros for advice but they are pretty garbage in the ladies department.

"Show her your b-ball skills," Mario advised. "Dunking—that'll impress her."

"Whatever," scoffed Marcus. "Dedicate your next home run to her. Girls love that kinda stuff. That's how I got Maribel Sosa to go out with me. Just make sure you don't whiff."

But, homers and dunks hadn't gotten Daniela's attention yet. That's why I was stoked to see her new app. It was a sure-fire way to get to know her. It was just the in I needed!

Chapter Seven

SUSPECT NUMBER ONE
☞ Andrea Hackenpack

My campaign events were in full swing. My first talk, *Tutoring your Way to the Top* had spotty attendance. My second, a lunchtime Q & A called *Get on the Fast Track* with Hackenpack, had a few more attendees.

"Are there any other questions on how you can make the most of your time with your guidance counsellor?"

"When do you talk about camping?" asked Rocks Mudman from the back row.

"Yeah, aren't you here to tell us how to hack down a tree with a handsaw and pack for a week in a national park?" said Ed Nojna.

"This isn't what I thought it was going to be," announced Alberta Vincent as she got up. "I thought we were getting a free lunch pack, or backpack, or hacky sack. Something free."

It was time to end the session.

"Thanks for coming. Vote Andrea!" I called as they left the room.

"Hack and pack. Chopping down a tree and then building a log cabin in Algonquin National Park. What else would this Q &A be about?" muttered Ed as he left. I didn't have the time to explain the Dutch roots of my name because there was an alert on my phone. I got one! A real one! I grabbed my phone and ran to tell Jenny.

My app had been up and running for a few days. Harold had set up an *inbox* which pinged every time I received a question. Until now, only the J.R. Wilcott jokesters had written. Some wannabe comics just quickly rattled off a question:

Hey Bossypants, Why did the chicken cross the road?

Others obviously spent a lot of time formulating fake questions.

Dear Bossypants,

I have a humongous problem that keeps me up all night long. I fall asleep during class because I've been up thinking about it so much. In fact, I needed four stitches last week when I dozed off in music class and my head hit my tuba. I am desperate. Please, help me solve this problem so I can go back to having a good night's sleep! Why is Principal Losman so foxy?

My advice to them was to get a hobby. (This last person would have been perfect for the paper if it hadn't been shut down. The question was dumb but the grammar was perfect!) Some of the questions I received weren't even questions at all.

Dear Bossypants, I am thinking about burping the national anthem at our next basketball game. Belching rules!

Finally, a real question sat buzzing in my inbox. I raced down the hall towards the cafeteria. My promise of confidentiality meant I couldn't read Jenny the actual question but I could show her the flashing alert. I was just about to burst into the cafeteria when I saw Harold. Deep in conversation with someone, he didn't notice me. It must have been an important talk because their heads were bent low and they were whispering. In fact, I only recognized Harold because of the green argyle sweater vest he always wore. I knew it was rude to interrupt but I had to share my good news. Gently I tapped Harold on the shoulder.

"Guess what's in my..." I was too surprised finish my sentence. Staring back at me were Harold and *Marty Jenkins*.

"Hey, Andrea," mumbled Harold as he looked down at the floor. I got the distinct impression I had interrupted something important. Harold wouldn't look me in the eye—he was now suddenly staring at the ceiling—and Marty, not normally a good friend of mine, seemed thrilled to see me.

"In your?" prompted Marty. "You said something's in your...?"

"In...in my lunch bag today," I stammered. I wasn't sure what I had just walked in on, but my gut warned me not to reveal anything important. "A hot dog," I finally spat out. Quick thinking is usually one of my strengths but not today.

"Yep," I continued trying to make my story believable. "I know, I know. You're wondering how as-of-now former veggie, Andrea Hackenpack, can eat a meaty lunch— especially a meat full of nitrates. But I woke up this morning in the mood for a hot dog. And the heart wants what the heart wants."

Marty nodded enthusiastically accepting my silly story at face value. "Did you know that dogs are one of the staples of competitive eating, Andrea? The world record is 72 hot dogs in ten minutes. Awesome, right?" said Marty. "I was just offering Harold here some competitive eating lessons in return for some math tutoring."

"Marty's stuck on chapter eleven," revealed Harold.

Marty nodded sheepishly. "We'll talk about that later, bud. I gotta jet now. Meeting Anil Kapur. He's going to give me some help on my French dialogue in return for a lesson on downing 42 cupcakes in eight minutes." He gave Harold an awkward high five and sprinted off in the other direction.

Harold turned to me. His shifty eyes and secretive expression were gone. He looked me straight in the eye and smiled. "That was a close one but I don't think he noticed a thing. Nice save with the hotdogs, by the way. Any mention of food distracts Marty. So what is it really? Problem with the app?" asked Harold. He looked concerned. "Is there something you're unhappy with? I've got some free time right now and we can fix whatever's wrong."

He was so friendly and helpful! I chalked up my earlier suspicion to nerves and gave into my excitement. "I've got my first real *Bossypants* question," I told him proudly as I held up the phone. It was flashing again.

"Hey!" I must have missed the *ping*. Now I had two questions in my inbox!

"That's great, Andrea," said Harold sincerely. "Glad to know the app is working and people are using it. Let me know if there's anything else you need help with."

"Thanks, Harold." I was glad I had confided in Harold. He was a good guy to have in my corner. I waved goodbye to him and headed the other way. Lunch would have to wait as I had some advice to give!

Chapter Eight

SUSPECT NUMBER TWO
☞ Ralph Dorph

My own smartphone was charging so I borrowed Mara's. I downloaded the advice app, logged in and got right to the point.

Dear Bossypants,

Can you give me some advice on how to make some good friends?

From,

New to Wilcott

I wasn't sure what kind of response I would get. At best, I would get some solid suggestions and have lunch mates within the week. At worst, I would learn a little bit about J.R. Wilcott's sense of humour.

Mara's phone vibrated a few hours later. "It's all yours," she said as she handed it to me.

Excited, I clicked on the icon and read what Bossypants had to say.

"Read it out loud," my sister demanded.

"If you want me to," I mumbled. I wasn't so sure about Bossypants's advice. Mara nodded enthusiastically so I read:

Dear N.T.W.,

Don't worry. Your problem is a common one that many people experience. It can definitely be rough but I know how to help you.

"Confident yet sympathetic," said Mara approvingly. "Go on, Ralphie."

Focus on making a good first (or second or third) impression. You need to pull out all the stops if you want to come away with your heart's desire. Flowers and candy are a start. Everyone loves a box of chocolates. But if you really want to charm, you need to seal the deal with an extravagant gesture. Have you thought about writing a poem? Wear your heart on your sleeve and express how you feel. And if you have the confidence, deliver your poem in a public place. That will surely leave a lasting and winning impression!

Good luck, N.T.W. Send me a progress ping.

Bossypants

"Kinda weird, don't you think?" I asked my sister nervously. I wasn't sure about sending chocolates to the tall guy who lent me a pen in history class or flowers to the girl who showed me where the bathroom was on my first day of school.

Mara re-read the mail I had written to Bossypants. "Well, Bossypants is definitely a girl. There's no doubting that. And a girl who has a romantic view of the world. I think she really focused on the fact that you didn't ask her how to find some guys to hang out with. You asked her how to make *good* friends."

"That's true," I said slowly. "But isn't her advice a bit over-the-top?"

"In Bossypants's world, a friend is a soul mate. And you need to be a bit over-the-top if you're going to find your soul-mate in the daily grind of middle school."

"So you think I should take her advice?" I was still unconvinced.

"Well, I do agree that it's over the top, but Bossypants knows more about J.R.Wilcott than we do. Maybe this is the kind of thing that works there. You're eating your lunch alone, Ralphie. You've got nothing to lose. I promise to help you write a banging poem."

Mara was right. I had nothing to lose. I went to find my rhyming dictionary.

Chapter Nine

SUSPECT NUMBER THREE
☞ Joe Jacobs

I spent an hour writing to Daniela "Bossypants" Olafson — 45 minutes more than I usually spend on homework.

"Ma, does *gorgeous* have one *r* or two?" I yelled from the top of the stairs. I really wanted to get this right. "What's another word for *awesome red hair*?" I called out a few minutes later.

My hollering caught my brothers' attention. Mario and Marcus burst through my door to see what I was doing. Soon, the suggestions were flying back and forth.

"*Ravishing* is a good one," offered Mario. "Just make sure you spell it right. You don't want to tell her she is *radishing*. In my experience, girls don't like to be compared to vegetables."

"Be romantic but not drippy," advised Marco. "Compare her to a bases-loaded home run—a grand slam! Grando salami!"

In the end, my brothers helped me write an awesome email. It revealed exactly how I felt about Daniela Olafsson. I downloaded the app to Mario's phone and sent my message.

Dear Bossypants,

How can I impress a girl I really like a lot?

Yours truly,

New To Women

Then I went downstairs for dinner. Mario's phone pinged as I made my way through my second plate of spaghetti and extra-meat-filled meatballs. By this time, my whole family knew about Bossypants. Everyone stopped slurping their pasta.

"Come on, what did she say?" asked my mom impatiently.

I clicked on the app and read aloud.

Dear N.T.W.

It can be tough to make a special connection in all the hustle and bustle of school. Start by focusing on your interests and work from there. J.R. Wilcott has many extra-curricular activities. What kinds of things do you like to do? Sports? Drama? Try joining the chess club and striking up a conversation with your opponent. Things will flow naturally if you are feeling comfortable.

Good luck, N.T.W. Send me a progress ping.

Bossypants

"Whatdaya think?" I said as I put the phone down.

"She's definitely into you!" said Marco smiling.

"Totally!" crowed Mario.

"I think she's telling you to join the chess club," remarked my dad dryly.

"Why don't you surprise her?" suggested my mom. "Present her with some pink roses before you start your first match."

I gave it some thought. "You're right, Dad. Daniela isn't really sporty. The chess club makes more sense than intramural basketball. And, Ma, that's a great idea." I stopped for a moment. "But I know nothing about chess."

"Not a problem," said Mario. "I just so happen to have a beginner's chess app on my phone."

We all looked at him.

"I also have a redhead I'm trying to impress. And not just because her hair reminds me of the hockey net goal light," revealed my big brother. "She likes reading and chess—maybe even reading about chess. I'm not sure."

"Crazy!" laughed Marcus as me and my bros excused ourselves from the table.

"Think you can set a pick and roll in chess?" asked Marcus as we headed upstairs.

"Not sure," said Mario. "But hopefully you can dunk a few of the pieces."

"No food fights tonight. And all because of chess. Now that's crazy," marvelled my mom.

"There's hope for them after all," said my dad. "Just don't tempt fate by making baked potatoes tomorrow night!"

I could hear them laughing as me and my bros got down to business.

Chapter Ten

SUSPECT NUMBER ONE
☞ Andrea Hackenpack

My first two clients were fairly straightforward: a lonely kid who was new to Wilcott and a guy with a crush on a girl. Easy! I recommended the newbie join a club and I suggested the lovelorn guy make a grand gesture that would capture the attention of his crush. Then I waited to hear back from the two. If this worked out, I'd have a swarm of followers in no time. President A. Hackenpack: it had the perfect ring to it.

Chapter Eleven

SUSPECT NUMBER TWO
☞ Ralph Dorph

Today was the big day. I still had major doubts about holding a poetry reading in a public place. The idea seemed over the top and embarrassing. Maybe I had misunderstood Bossypants's advice? I re-read the email a thousand times. But, no matter how hard I tried, I couldn't come up with another meaning for *deliver your poem in a public place.*

"Your new school sounds a bit crazy," said my mom.

"I like it," said my dad. "It sounds like a classic school for the arts—with kids standing on tables reading poems, breaking into song in the middle of math class and grabbing their band instruments and having random jam sessions."

"Do not, under any circumstances, stand on a table when you read your poem, Ralphie," demanded my mom. "You've had bad balance ever since that middle-ear infection."

Despite my nagging doubt, Mara and I wrote a poem together. I practised it again and again until I felt comfortable— or as comfortable as I could get reading homemade poetry to all of my new classmates. Mara thought it would be best if I delivered my poem during lunch time.

"For maximum effect," she explained as she poured milk over her cereal.

I was too nervous to eat breakfast.

Mara gave me a hug. "Don't worry so much, Ralphie. We wrote a killer rhyme that will charm the whole school. You'll be fighting off all your new friends by the end of the day. Just remember to talk loudly and enunciate."

It was hard to concentrate during math class and impossible to remember a word my history teacher said. All I could focus on was the clock. It was inching its way to 11:30am. Lunch time! I really hoped Bossypants knew what she was talking about. Spouting poems as the other kids ate their tuna sandwiches wouldn't have gone over well at Shaker Heights Middle School. I would have been laughed out of the cafeteria at L'Ecole du Paris Nord. And they would have pelted me with sushi at Fujita International School.

Lost in my own thoughts, I didn't hear the bell ring. But the *thud* of text books slamming shut and the *scrape* of chairs being pushed back snapped me back to reality. It was lunch time for the rest of J.R. Wilcott. For me it was showtime. Butterflies were starting to commandeer my stomach. I thought about taking the long way to the cafeteria but my legs were beginning to wobble. It was best to go straight there before I chickened out.

No one noticed as I nervously walked through the cafeteria doors. A few kids glanced my way as I pushed back a chair. A few more eyes turned in my direction as I climbed onto the table. I hoped the other kids couldn't hear my heart pounding—it felt like it was about to burst out of my chest.

After what seemed to be the longest second of my life, I found myself standing on top of a lunch table, looking down at the grade sixes, sevens and eights that made up J.R.Wilcott Middle School. They had all put down their sandwiches. Silently, they stared at me. I stared back, mute with fear. They were waiting for me to do something. Out of the corner of my eye, I could see Mr. Papernick heading my way. Mr. Kagan grabbed him by the arm and stopped him. It was now or never. I prayed my vocal chords would work.

"Hi. I'm Ralph," I mumbled. "I'm new here."

"Did he just say he was going to ralph?" shouted a panicked voice from the back of the room.

Mara was right. I needed to talk loudly and clearly. Still trembling, I unfolded a piece of paper and began to read.

"Here's a poem I wrote for you guys. I hope you like it.
My name is Ralph Dorph and I've just moved to town.
I'm not a star athlete or the class clown.
At first I seem a little quiet and shy.
It's not always easy being the new guy.

Because of my dad's work, this is my fourth middle school.
Hopefully some of you think that is incredibly cool.
My likes include comics, movies and chicken wings
But I'm open to experiencing all different things.
I'd like the chance to get to know all of you
And learn things about Wilcott like if I should avoid the
   lamb stew.

I could hear some giggles. Hoping these were laughs of appreciation, I stopped and looked up from my paper. To my relief, everyone was smiling. I couldn't help but notice a very tall guy—I'm pretty sure he was the same guy who lent me a pencil last week—nodding his head enthusiastically as he scribbled on a piece of paper.

Smiling back at my classmates, I finished my poem.

Hopefully I've won you with the spoken word
And you don't think I am a giant nerd.
So if you are interested in hanging with Ralph Dorph
Let me know and we can go to the mall or the wharf.

I wasn't thrilled with the end of my poem— I had no idea if there was a wharf nearby— but it was next to impossible to come up with a word that rhymed with Dorph. It didn't seem to matter though. I performed a little dab to signal I was finished and the room broke out in applause. The poem was a hit! A slew of hands shot out to help me down from the table.

"There's no wharf around here, but we can go to the movies if you like," said a girl with green glasses.

"I love wings, too, dude!" said a guy called Rocks Mudman, offering me a piece of chicken.

"Listen to me," said another guy, "and avoid the beef stroganoff. Every Wednesday they serve that slop!"

Bossypants was a genius! I would no longer be dining alone!

Chapter Twelve

SUSPECT NUMBER ONE
☞ Andrea Hackenpack

"How cool was that?" said Jenny as we watched the new guy climb down from the table and get swallowed up by a sea of chatty Wilcotters.

"He's kind of cute in a skinny kind of way," observed Marlene Tang.

Jenny nodded vigorously. "Quite cute if you imagine him without the plaid turtleneck. All he needs is a quick, guided trip to the mall."

I wasn't really listening to them. "In the land of emails, texts and Instagram, poetry has made a comeback," I mused to no one in particular.

I had a good feeling about the advice I had just doled out on my app. I recommended my lovelorn client use poetry to win a girl's heart. Now this new guy, Ralph Dorph, was using poetry to make friends. My words of wisdom were spot on! My wannabe Romeo would definitely win the girl of his dreams via poetry.

"I'm a genius. A trend-setting genius," I said louder than I meant to.

Jenny looked sharply at me. Then she noticed a surly-looking Marty Jenkins.

"Looks like Marty's been sucking on a lemon," she said pointing to my left. "Or he has a major hate on for rhyming stanzas."

"Jealous much?" laughed Marlene.

We were interrupted by a loud tapping sound. Mr. Kagan was standing on the same table where Ralph had just stood. He was using his foot to get our attention.

"Settle down! Settle down," he bellowed over the lunchtime din. "First, I want to offer a warm welcome to Ralph Dorph. Ralph, you're going to love it at J.R. Wilcott Middle School. The kids here are smart, funny and friendly." Mr. Kagan paused for a moment as a few kids hooted and clapped. Then he continued, "Ralph's poem inspired me. And, judging by your reaction, I think you're all feeling inspired, too. With that in mind, I've come up with a fabulous idea."

"This cannot be good," muttered Jenny as the room quieted to a still.

"We're going to hold a poetry slam every week. Every

Wednesday, ten or twelve kids will recite their own poetry. Then we'll vote on the best. Let's call it Wild Wordy Wednesday!"

If he was expecting the cafeteria to break out in applause, he had the wrong room.

"Wild Wordy Wednesday?" repeated a kid from grade seven. "More like Mid-week Misery."

"How can I concentrate on eating my lunch if I have to listen to poetry all the time?" asked Daryl Talleyman with tomato sauce dribbling down his chin.

"Do we have to do this?" asked Marlene getting right to the point.

"I think it's a wonderful idea," echoed Ms. Chronopolis, Wilcott's new drama teacher. "It will help develop your oral presentation skills. I've got some wiggle room on my syllabus so I'll incorporate Wild Wordy Wednesday into your final grade. It will be great fun!"

Her pep talk failed to light up the room. The grumbling grew louder. It was one thing to listen to a little poem from the new guy, but it was another thing to be stuck writing one yourself. And it was a completely different—and supremely annoying—ball of wax to stand on a cafeteria table, read it aloud and be graded on it!

"It will be great fun," repeated Mr. Kagan undeterred. His tone was cheerful but he meant business. "I'll create a sign-up sheet today. You'll all have a chance to wow the school—just like Ralph."

Everyone had forgotten about Ralph Dorph—until now! A jam-packed room of resentful eyes turned towards him.

"Ugh. Take a long walk off a short wharf, Dorph," said the girl with green glasses.

Rocks Mudman took back his chicken wings. The sea of people surrounding Ralph parted until he was standing alone.

Chapter Thirteen

SUSPECT NUMBER THREE
☞ Joe Jacobs

Wilcotters are weird. First everyone was all over this Ralph Dorph guy like he had made the game-winning free throw. Then no one would even look at him—as if he had just shanked the tie-breaking field goal. And a few dudes, like Wormald and Jenkins, were laughing like it was the funniest thing they had ever seen.

Me? I wanted to talk to this Ralph. He was an ace rhymer and there was a good chance I'd need his help. Marcus told me that girls love when guys write them poetry, especially when it's about their hair. I was pretty sure Ralph could help me find a word that rhymed with *awesome, red and long*. His poem was the bomb. Everyone loved it before Kagan stuck his nose in. I like our English teacher but sometimes he reminded me of my old little league coach—a classic over-manager. Repeated visits to the mound can screw things up for a struggling pitcher. He should have just left Ralph and his poem alone.

I noticed yesterday that a Ralph Dorph had signed up for the chess club. At the time, I had no idea what a Ralph Dorph was. Now I knew. He was the Cy Young of rhymers. I stood up. The chess club met in five minutes.

"See you guys at basketball practice," I said to my tablemates.

"Where are you going?" asked my good friend and fellow point guard, Anil Kapur.

"Chess club," I said shovelling the rest of my pastrami sub in my mouth.

"Stress tub?" repeated Jeremy Margles. "Don't be so hard on yourself, buddy! Everyone misses a penalty shot now and then."

I didn't have time to correct him. My first unofficial date with Daniela was less than four minutes away and I needed to make a quick pit stop at my locker to grab the pink roses I stashed there. Hopefully they hadn't gotten crushed under my baseball glove. I needed to have an ace-in-the-hole ready for Daniela.

"These flowers are for you, Daniela." Too boring.

"You are the pitcher to my catcher, D!" Too much.

"I hope you like these flowers. I tried to match them to your hair." Not bad.

I was so busy trying to perfect my first pitch that I didn't see Harold Wormald before it was too late.

"Sorry, man," I said helping him up off the floor. "Wasn't paying enough attention."

He looked annoyed. "It's fine, Joe."

I scooped up his textbooks and tried to make conversation. "How's everything going?"

"Busy. Test last period," said Harold relaxing a bit. "Literary terms. I'm just going over them right now. Homonyms, homophones, antonyms, synonyms, etcetera. Basic stuff I should ace...easy, peasy, one, two, three or should I say *won, too, free*?"

Harold took one look at me and could tell I had no idea what he was talking about.

"Classic homophones! Two or more words pronounced alike but different in meaning or spelling." He looked annoyed when I still didn't get it. "You should have learned this in Grade Six, Joe. Hi/high, aloud/allowed, be/bee. I could go on forever if I had the time."

Harold was one smart dude. I thought about asking him to find a romantic way to say *all-you-can-eat buffet* but he rushed off before I could open my mouth.

I was running late. I jogged down to Room 202 where the chess club usually met. But when I got there I couldn't find Daniela. There were a few blonds, a lot of brunettes and tons of pocket protectors but no red-heads. I waited and waited with my flowers but Daniela never showed. Maybe I had misunderstood her advice. Maybe *try joining the chess club and striking up a conversation with your opponent* really meant go to the bowling alley and knock down all the pins on the first try. Or maybe she was really shy and chickened out at the last moment. I gave up on Daniela and looked for Ralph Dorph instead. Maybe we could work on a poem in between chess moves? There were plaid turtlenecks everywhere but no sign of Ralph. No Daniela and no Ralph. Strike one and strike two. Dejected, I pitched my flowers to the nearest wide receiver in sight.

"Well, Mr. Jacobs," said Mr. Papernick catching the bouquet, "I love an arrangement of roses as much as anyone, but don't think this gets you out of tomorrow's algebra quiz."

I nodded quickly at him. With no Daniela and no Ralph, I needed to find another chess partner. I looked around but everyone had already paired up.

"Looks like it's you and me, Mr. Jacobs," said Mr. Papernick as he set up the board. "I can quiz you on algebraic equations in between moves if you like. Think of it as thanks for the flowers—pink roses are Mrs. Papernick's favourite!"

Ugh, a chess date with Mr. Papernick! My romantic afternoon was officially a bottom of the ninth, three runs down, bases-loaded strikeout.

Chapter Fourteen

SUSPECT NUMBER TWO
☞ Ralph Dorph

"I heard it didn't go very well," said my mom as we sat down for dinner. "I made chicken wings to cheer you up."

"I never want to see those horrible things again." I shuddered. It would take quite a bit of time before I could enjoy poultry again.

"Why don't you compose an apologetic poem?" suggested my dad. "*I hope you accept my humblest apology and be my partner in third period biology.* You can deliver it on the next Wild Wordy Wednesday."

"It's not funny, Mara!" I said glaring at my giggling sister. "After school, I saw some kid pointing at me."

"Well, that's a good start," said my mother. "Now people know who you are."

"No, mom, it's not good. He was pointing me out as poetry-loving nerd, Real Dork. Now I'd give anything to be anonymous Ralph Dorph."

"I'm sorry, Ralphie," Mara said turning serious. "We'll come up with a plan and make this right."

"I think you should write to Bossypants again," said my dad. "Her advice wasn't totally off base. The kids loved your poem. They just didn't like Wild Wordy Wednesday. Wild Wordy Wednesday is what did you in. Wild Wordy Wednesday is the culprit."

"Stop!" I cringed every time he mentioned Mr. Kagan's *fabulous idea*. "I can't hear those three words again."

My father paused for a second. "It was Triple Dub's fault. Write to Bossypants and see what she advises."

I looked to Mara who was nodding. "I think that's the best plan we have. Write to Bossypants and see what she says. This time we won't take her advice if we don't like it."

The dinner table was full of nodding faces so I took out my phone and began to type.

Chapter Fifteen

SUSPECT NUMBER ONE
☞ Andrea Hackenpack

I had the feeling that good news (via a great progress ping) was right around the corner. The J.R. Wilcott presidency was in my grasp and the ultimate goal, Fitzpatrick All-Girls Private High School, was so close I could almost grab it.

I planned my evening as I walked home from school: a few hours studying, a phone call to Jenny, and then forty-five minutes on the drums. After, I would reward myself with something crazy like ice cream or an episode of reality TV. It was shaping up to be a great night! My intricate planning was interrupted by a ping. I searched for my phone frantically. I assumed it was a progress ping and I couldn't wait to hear about my client's success. My hands trembled with excitement as I clicked on the Bossypants app (™!). Two emails sat in my inbox! This was truly amazing. Ice cream and reality TV tonight! I scanned the first email quickly. Overcome with dizziness, I sat down on the curb. I opened the second email and read. Suddenly I felt like I was suffocating. Unable to catch my breath, I lay down on the grass and tried not to hyperventilate. Perhaps I misunderstood the emails? Maybe I was confused by the tone? Had I overlooked the sarcasm? Just to be sure, I reread the first message aloud.

Dear Bossypants

I took your advice and it didn't work. In fact, it backfired. Now I really have no friends. Do you have any other ideas? I'd prefer something a little more low-key this time if possible. Thanks,

New To Wilcott

No, I was confident I hadn't misunderstood anything. This client was unhappy! Flabbergasted, I read the next mail aloud.

Hey Bossypants,

I took your advice but no dice. I still haven't gotten a date with you (know who.) What should I do now?

xoxo

N.T.W.

This mail was punctuated with a sad face—there was no misunderstanding here. I tried to stand up but I was still lightheaded. Why couldn't I remember any of my breathing exercises? I decided to stay where I was for the time being. My thoughts were clouded by shock so it was difficult to make sense of the situation. But one thing was clear— solving this crisis would take some serious strategizing. And there was no time like the present—even if I was lying on Mrs. McGillicuddy's lawn—to begin brainstorming.

I tried accessing my Sent Mail to reread my original messages to see if there was some way my clients misunderstood my advice, but the folder wasn't loading. It didn't take me long to compose the perfect advice for my wannabe Romeo but it took me much longer to send it. The app was malfunctioning and, though I pressed send 112 times, my response to lovelorn N.T.W. still sat sadly in my outbox. I tried calling Harold for help but he wasn't answering his phone. I knew I had composed the most perfect words of wisdom but they were uselessly stuck on my side of the app. I reread my advice, triple-checking for any spelling mistakes in between my frustrated attempts to send the email.

Dear N.T.W.,

I'm sorry my last advice didn't work. Promise me that you won't give up! There is a lot at stake here and these things take time. You mustered up the courage to express yourself last time and you need to do it again. I always say that it is important to be noticed and discussed—this is also true when pursuing a girl. Here's how to make yourself unforgettable to her.

It is crucial that you get to know the girl of your dreams. You need to find somewhere the two of you can meet. Does she have a special table in the cafeteria? Talk to her there casually but don't grill her. Find out her likes and dislikes— coax it out of her. For example, where was she on the weekend? What kind of things does she choose to do in her free time? Does she like quiet walks and lazy Sundays? Then spring into action. Wow her with flowers—they are tough to beat. Go all out! Show off your muscles if you think they are impressive. Be smooth and cheesy! Leak some details about yourself and see her reaction. All girls are not the same, N.T.W. Different girls like different things so perhaps, to cover your bases, combine all of my suggestions. This is just my two cents. But have confidence in yourself and put in your own two cents, too. You'll score a date in no time. I'm sure you'll make a great pair!

Good luck, N.T.W. Send me a progress ping. I relish hearing about her reaction.

Bossypants

I kept calling Harold. There must have been a big math test coming up because he didn't answer his phone. In between calls, I drafted a response to my other client who was still looking to make friends. I didn't hear back from Harold until the next day. When he finally answered the telephone I tried to hide my irritation as he apologized for being unreachable.

"I'm sorry, Andrea," he said. I could hear a boy's voice laughing in the background and Harold trying to hush him. "Little brothers are the worst," he added.

He promised to get the app fixed as soon as possible.

Chapter Sixteen

SUSPECT NUMBER THREE
☞ Joe Jacobs

I was positive I'd hear from Bossypants right after I wrote to her. She was pretty good at getting back to me quickly. But by dinnertime I still hadn't heard from her.

"Why hasn't she written back?" I asked my family as I grabbed a few pork chops.

"Maybe she didn't understand my email? I should have been more straightforward," I said as I helped myself to baked potatoes.

"Ma, you know women, give me some advice!" I demanded as I buttered a handful of rolls.

"Relax and enjoy your dinner," advised my mother.

"I bet she's taking her time trying to plan the perfect date," said Marcus as he drowned his pork chops in gravy.

"Love can't be rushed, little bro," chimed in Mario as he

snatched a roll from my plate.

As tough as it was, I tried to relax and enjoy my dinner. Even though I hadn't gotten a response by dessert, I managed to choke down a few slices of blueberry-rhubarb pie.

"More whipped cream, please," I requested glumly.

I sat down to watch the baseball game with my brothers. They tried their best to cheer me up.

"Freshly popped," said Marcus handing me a gigantic bowl of popcorn. "Extra butter and cinnamon just for you."

I used one hand to check the phone and the other to shovel popcorn in my mouth. But after a few dozen handfuls, I still hadn't gotten a ping. My stomach was starting to feel a bit weird and I couldn't concentrate on the game. Even though it was only the fifth inning, I decided to call it a night.

"See you guys in the morning," I mumbled as I checked my empty inbox one last time.

I still hadn't heard from Bossypants when I sat down for my morning pancakes.

"What's taking her so long?" I asked in between mouthfuls.

"I'm sure you'll hear from her by the end of first period," said my mom as she handed me the syrup.

Mario was cool enough to let me take his phone to school. "Just don't leave the ringer on in math class and get it confiscated," he warned.

First period was English. Mr. Kagan gave us the hour to catch up on our assignments. Cool! It would be easy to sneak peeks at the phone. I hadn't started the book report due next week. Actually, I hadn't even gotten past the third chapter of the novel. It's hard to read and watch playoff hockey at the same time. After checking my empty inbox one last time, I cracked open the book. But after reading the same sentence five times, I gave up. I grabbed a pen and took a run at writing a poem. I worked pretty hard for the next half hour and managed to find words that rhymed with *cute, homer* and *next weekend*. I was so into writing my poem that I didn't hear the bell ring.

"Come on, Joe," said Anil, lightly punching me in the arm.

I grabbed my bag and headed into the hallway but my mind was elsewhere. What rhymed with *my brother can drive us*? Suddenly I felt my pocket vibrate. It could only be one thing. I dropped my bag and grabbed the phone. Finally!

Dear N.T.W.,

I'm sorry my last advice didn't work. But don't give up! There is a lot at steak here and these things take thyme. You mustard up the courage to express yourself last time and you need to do it again. I always say that it is important to be noticed and disgust—this is also true when pursuing a girl. Here's how to make yourself unforgettable to her.

It is crucial that you to get to know the girl of your dreams.

You need to find somewhere the two of you can meat. Does she have a special table in the cafeteria? Talk to her there casually but don't grill her. Find out her likes and dislikes—Cokes it out of her. For example, where has she bean on the weekend? What kind of things does she chews to do in her free time? Does she like quiet woks and lazy sundaes? Then spring into action. Wow her with flours—they are tough to beet. Go all out. Show off your mussels if you think they are impressive. Be smooth and cheesy! Leek some details about yourself and see her reaction. All girls are not the same, N.T.W. Different girls like different things so perhaps, to cover your bases, combine all of my suggestions. This is just my two scents. But have confidence in yourself and put in your own two scents, too. You'll score a date in no time. I'm sure you'll make a great pear together!

Good luck, N.T.W. Send me a progress ping. I relish hearing about her reaction.

Bossypants

Awesome! Daniela wanted me to cook her a steak dinner with all the fixings. That was a little more in my wheelhouse than writing a goofy poem. I'd raid the fridge right tonight and see what we had—I was pretty sure my mom had leeks but I wasn't so sure about beets. Then I'd grill up a masterpiece and give it to her for lunch. I'd win her through her stomach. A girl with an appetite—I knew Daniela was perfect for me!

Chapter Seventeen

SUSPECT NUMBER TWO
☞ Ralph Dorph

I heard the ping as I walked down the hall but didn't stop to check my phone. I was running late and didn't want all eyes on me when I walked into history class. Everyone was still complaining about Wild Wordy Wednesday—I didn't want to call even more attention to myself.

People pretty much ignored me during lunch. On one hand, I guess it was better than being called Real Dork. But, on the other, I was still eating alone. I felt so low that even chess club seemed to be too much. I'd explain my absence to Mr. Papernick later. I nervously clicked on the advice app. Bossypants had turned me into a word nerd. This time, I would be careful before taking her advice.

Dear N.T.W.,

I'm sorry my last advice didn't work. But don't give up! Making good friends takes time. It sounds like you're shy. Despite being a wallflower, you need to step up your presents at school. Swim team, basketball team, school play... get out there and get yourself noticed and disgust!

In my experience, Wilcotters have a great sense of humour and love a good tees. Do you have a good sense of humour and appreciate a good practical joke? Find something to tees us with and I promise it will leave a lasting impression.

Go fourth and conquer!

Good luck, N.T.W. Send me a progress ping.

Bossypants

Step up my presents at school? Tees us? I was pretty sure she was telling me to go to the mall and buy gifts for my classmates. And then hand them out while I wore a cool t-shirt. Or maybe I was supposed to hand out t-shirts as presents? Her advice sounded weird although at least this time I wouldn't have to write a poem. Maybe she thought I should try to make up for the Wild Wordy Wednesday debacle with small tokens of appreciation for my classmates? The more I thought about it, the more it made sense. I could hand out a few presents that revealed a little bit about Ralph Dorph.

I reread Bossypants's mail. *Get yourself noticed and disgust.*

I guess Bossypants believed that all attention is good and there's no such thing as bad publicity. The presents seemed fairly straightforward, but how I was supposed to do all this and disgust my classmates. I'd have to give it some thought.

I went to my sock drawer after school to check out my present-buying funds. Ten dollars—it wouldn't get me far. I made a beeline for Mara's room. She had so many old t-shirts that they spilled out of her closet. And she had some weird bedazzler thing that made everything sparkle. That's where I would start. *Show my presents and tees.* It was doable. First things first, I needed to throw out all of my turtlenecks.

Chapter Eighteen

SUSPECT NUMBER ONE
☞ Andrea Hackenpack

I was getting curious about my clients. I might have let them down the first time, but I was positive I hit the mark now. Even though my app promised complete confidentiality, I tried to figure out who they were. The Bossypants app was available for all of Wilcott, so it was hard to tell if my clients were in my grade. I kept my eyes open and ears pealed hoping to hear about a new Wilcott couple or catch a fresh face playing horse with the basketball team.

Harold had fixed the app so my outbox finally cleared, but I still couldn't get my Sent Mail to load. He said it would take him more time to figure out what was wrong.

School elections were in a few weeks and I needed to bolster my campaign with successful clients. I had yet to post any fabulous testimonials because, so far, there weren't any good ones to post. I tried to improve my app by posting a few Top Ten lists. Jenny's *Top Ten Shoes to Wear to Your Math Test* got a few clicks. I also added a bulletin board where Wilcotters could post ideas they had to improve our school. Time was ticking! I hadn't gotten any new clients and had gained only a sprinkling of new followers. Currently, the app was the opposite of *noticed* and *discussed*. My original plan was to tell everyone I was Bossypants at the final speeches. But there was no point of a campaign-ending big reveal if there was nothing to reveal!

Marty was offering competitive-eating lessons to everyone in sight. Six medium-sized watermelons in eleven minutes. He was making himself noticed and discussed. And, in-between scarfing down massive amounts of fruit, he was offering Wilcotters extra periods in study-hall instead of Algebra, new checker boards so the chess club had something to do in their down time and goggles with Mp3 players built into them for the swim-team. He was covering all of his bases on land and in water. Gwenn Yoon was a low key candidate but still in the race. She wasn't as flashy as Marty—I wasn't exactly sure what she stood for—but she could still be dangerous. I had put all of my election eggs in one basket: being a true leader. And I needed the Bossypants app (™!) as proof.

Chapter Nineteen

SUSPECT NUMBER THREE
☞ Joe Jacobs

One steak dinner with all the fixings ready to serve! With the help of my family, it only took me four hours to make Daniela the awesomest meal of her dreams.

First, Marcus made a list of every food Bossypants mentioned in her email. "We don't want to leave anything important out," he said. Then we grabbed a 9 oz. steak from the freezer and fired up the grill. Mario heated up the wok. Supersized jars of mustard and relish were waiting in the fridge and I found thyme in the spice rack. Flour was in the pantry. We had three different types of cheese but none was super smooth. Hopefully mozzarella would be good enough.

"Ma, you got any leeks?" I hollered. "What about beets? And beans? Any mussel thingies?"

Sick of listening to me yell through the wall, my mom came into the kitchen. Quickly she scanned the list of ingredients. "Daniela's appetite rivals you three beasts. I wonder how much her family spends on groceries every week."

"Ma, the mussels," I said trying to get her to focus.

She looked at the list again. "I'm not sure about this, Joe. Mussels and steak? Surf and turf is usually with lobster. And I have my doubts about the cheese. And the—"

I looked at Mario. He knew how important this was to me.

"I'll go," he said grabbing the car keys. "I know what we need."

"Mussels are in the fish department," yelled my dad from the other room.

We were hauling out the deep fryer when Mario got home.

"We weren't sure what to do with the flour so we Googled it and found a recipe for deep-fried steak that uses flour and bread crumbs," I told him.

"Cool," said Mario as he unpacked the groceries. "I gotcha three different ice creams, hot fudge, nuts and whipped cream. Serve it at room temperature and you can drink it through a straw—the perfect lazy sundae! You'll have to make it again tomorrow, but we can put one together now and make sure it tastes good."

"Nice!" said Marcus. "One hand on the remote, one hand on dessert."

Mario unpacked the rest of the bag: four large leeks, two cans of lima beans, a six-pack of Coke and a big jar of Cheez Whiz.

"Smoothest cheese I know," he said.

It was getting steamy in the kitchen. Everyone was sweating up a storm. My dad manned the wok; Marcus worked the deep fryer as my mom washed the mussels; and Mario melted ice cream. I made sure we didn't miss any ingredients and provided everyone with squirts of Gatorade.

"Remember to add the lima beans, Marcus!"

"Why don't we put the Cheez Whiz in the blender, just to make sure it's super-smooth?"

"I think nuts will clog the straw, Mario."

It was a team effort and by the end of the night, a Jacobs homerun sat on the table.

- Deep-fried steak topped with a spicy mustard and sweet relish sauce (Mom and Marcus's creation)
- A puree of mussels and leeks (Mom tried to talk Marcus out of putting fish in the blender but my bro was positive his dish would be a smash right out of the ballpark)
- Stir-fried beets and lima beans in a Coca-Cola marinade (My dad's awesome idea)
- And a lukewarm sundae with a purple bendy straw in the middle courtesy of me and Mario.

"Put it in Tupperware right away so it doesn't go bad," advised my mom.

"Don't forget the most important ingredient!" said my dad excitedly. He handed me the jar of Cheez Wiz. "Put it in your backpack now so you don't forget it tomorrow."

"Her meal will be smooth and cheesy as requested," promised Marcus as Mario nodded in agreement. "There's no way she won't love it!"

Chapter Twenty

SUSPECT NUMBER ONE
☞ Andrea Hackenpack

My eyes and ears were tuned to a supersonic level, but I still hadn't noticed any new couplings in the halls of Wilcott. I checked with Jenny just in case I had somehow missed something.

"Not much new on the gossip front," she confirmed as we sat down for lunch. "It's been a very dry semester. I thought Marlene might ask out the new guy who loves turtlenecks, but then Wild Wordy Wednesday happened and now he's *persona non grata*. I've noticed a few guys acting a bit weird. Rumour has it Joe Jacobs asked Coach Carron if he could skip basketball practice so he could play in a chess match against Whitner—" She stopped suddenly and scrunched up her face. "Hey what's that smell?"

I noticed it too, and quickly covered my nose. It wasn't the usual odour of overcooked pasta and undercooked broccoloaf that wafted through the cafeteria. It was sharper and spicier. Gingerly, I sniffed again. The smell reminded me a bit of my dad. In fact, it reminded me of my dad, with a dollop of my grandpa and a dash of my Uncle Barry thrown in. It was overpowering. I pinched my nose discretely but it didn't help. The smell was getting sharper by the second, like it was coming closer and closer.

"It's Joe!" whispered Jenny to me. "I think he's OD'd on the aftershave."

"It smells like he washed his hair with cologne," I whispered back. "My grandpa Hackenpack's cologne."

"There's only one reason a guy does that," said Jenny knowingly. "The dating desert that has been Wilcott is getting some much needed rain. Tropical thunderstorm Jacobs is about to hit." Jenny knew much more about dating than I did. "Shh," she said hushing me. "Let's see what he tells his friends."

I craned my neck for a better view and watched Joe unpack a boatload of Tupperware from his knapsack.

Anil was the first to say something. "Bro had a little accident with the aftershave this morning?"

Joe laughed. "Girls love when you have your own two scents so I made an awesome mix of Marcus's cologne and Mario's aftershave. It smells good, right?"

"Well, it smells. That's for sure," said Anil shaking his

head good naturedly. "Are you taking dating advice from your brothers again?"

Joe didn't answer. He was preoccupied with opening his Tupperware. From what I could see, he had three little red jars, four medium-sized blue containers and a bottle of thick orange goop. Joe started with the little jars first. Then he opened one of the blue boxes. A new stench immediately enveloped the cafeteria.

"Ugh, Joe, that stinks!" cried out Anil.

At first sniff, their teammate, Jonah Isaacs, leaped under the table for cover.

Joe tried to coax him back. "It's nothing to be afraid of, buddy. Just some super-exclusive food I made yesterday. I have it on good authority that girls love this kind of chow."

"Told you this was all about a girl," whispered Jenny.

"Joe, you're not planning on having someone eat this?" asked a worried Anil.

Joe was opening more jars and the smells were getting progressively stinkier.

"I thought it smelled a little funky, too, at first," said Joe. "But, you get used to it. Girls just have different taste buds. You and I like PB & J but girls like classier things."

I wondered who the target was. Hopefully she had a cold and couldn't smell very well today. If she was lucky, she had a sore throat that would mask the unpleasant tastes which were sure to accompany these crazy concoctions. By now, Jenny and I had swiveled our chairs around so we could have a clear view of Joe. First he put what appeared to be a slab of fried chicken in the middle of a pink plate. He added a dollop of a chunky yellow and green glop on top.

"It's deep-fried," said Jenny, "but it doesn't smell like any chicken I've ever eaten. And that ain't ketchup on top!" Gingerly I took a sniff and instantly agreed with her.

Next he dug deep into the red Tupperware and scooped up a portion of red and green mush. "It looks gross but it kind of smells like Coke," remarked Jenny as Joe deposited the mush beside the deep-fried something-or-other.

I had to cover my nose when he added the last element to the plate. Although it was a drab grey colour, the stench was anything but dull. The smell was fishy but it didn't remind me of the salmon or tuna that was often on the Hackenpack dinner table. Looking closer, I thought I could spot some flecks of green in the mess. Whatever it was, the odor was potent—it nearly overpowered Joe's two scents!

Luckily, the next dish smelled like ice cream. Jenny and I watched in a fascinated silence as Joe combined a scoop of vanilla, two scoops of strawberry and a scoop of mint-chocolate chip in a little bowl. Then he drizzled a healthy portion of hot fudge on top and added a sprinkling of crushed nuts. He finished the sundae with a cloud of whipped cream.

"Now he's on track," I whispered to Jenny. "Ice cream is a good tactic."

"If he serves it cold," muttered Jenny. "What is he doing? He's just letting it all melt!"

We looked on as Joe's sundae turned into a rainbow-coloured puddle. We weren't the only ones staring.

"Joe, buddy, what are you doing?" asked an exasperated Anil. "You just let four good scoops go to waste."

Joe just smiled. He grabbed his dishes and stood up. "Time to get myself noticed and disgust her," he said to Isaac and Anil.

Usually I was all for getting yourself noticed and discussed, but I had serious doubts this was the kind of attention Joe craved. I wasn't sure who *her* was but there was no way she couldn't notice this train-wreck on a plate.

"Wish me luck," said Joe over his shoulder as he crossed the cafeteria.

Chapter Twenty-one

SUSPECT NUMBER THREE
☞ Joe Jacobs

My steak was a thing of deep-fried beauty. My beet n' bean stir fry was crackling. Although it was stinky, the mussels and leeks were looking good. And my sundae was melting to a lazy perfection. It was time to make my move. Bobbing and weaving through cafeteria traffic, I jogged over to Daniela's table. I was about to set the tray of food down in front of her when I realized there was no way I could give her this steak dinner. Not a chance! Nope, I had to shut it down. I jogged back across the room.

I had almost forgotten the most important ingredient! Back at my table I grabbed the orange bottle. Quickly I plastered Cheez Whiz all over the plate. Now everything was smooth and cheesy as requested! I thought about adding a smear of cheese to the sundae but Anil shook his head. I grabbed the food and headed back Daniela's way. This would be way better than the bagel she was chowing down on.

Chapter Twenty-two

SUSPECT NUMBER TWO
☞ Ralph Dorph

I was so wrapped up in my *presents and tees* project that I forgot to bring my lunch to school. It sat in the refrigerator at home as I sat alone in a corner of the cafeteria. My stomach was grumbling but there was nothing I could do about it. I didn't know anybody well enough to ask for half of their sandwich. And I had no money in my backpack. The cafeteria's French onion soup smelled good but I had no way of getting myself a bowl. I reached down into my backpack one last time hoping to come up with some loose change. I came up empty but maybe it was for the best. The smell of French onion soup had suddenly been replaced with a creepy deep-fried fishy smell. Out of the corner of my eye I saw a really tall guy—I'm pretty sure it was the same one who had lent me a pen—put a large tray of food in front of a girl with long red hair.

The smell was so strong that I found myself straining to get a better look at what could be on that tray. The stench captured all of my classmates' imaginations, too. There were more people watching this than Wild Wordy Wednesday.

"Special lunch today—a steak dinner, just the way you like it," announced the tall guy to the girl. She looked confused. "A steak dinner with all the fixings," he repeated. "All your favourites made for you by me."

I was pretty confused, too. He said it was steak but the whole plate was orange, lumpy and goopy.

"You made this just for me?" asked the red-headed girl trying to make sense of the situation. The tall guy nodded enthusiastically. He was grinning from ear to ear.

The girl stared at the plate. She still looked confused. "Thanks—I think," she finally said politely. But her fork remained on the table and her hands held on to her bagel for dear life.

"It's super cheesy so you have to eat it soon before it gets all soggy," implored the tall guy.

The red-headed girl looked nervous but she put down her bagel and picked up the fork.

"Daniela, are you sure about this?" whispered the guy beside her. "He says it's steak but it's orange and it reeks!"

"Yeah, think twice about this," begged a curly-haired girl sitting across the table. "I've never smelled any steak like this before."

Daniela didn't look sure about anything but the tall guy still stood there with a huge, hopeful grin on his face. He reminded me of my dog, Thurman, when he was a new pup. I almost wanted to eat the steak myself just to keep him looking so cheerful. The sane alternative was to dump the stinky steak into the nearest garbage can. But then the goofy grin would disappear. Daniela must have felt the same way because she cut a piece of the sunset-coloured meat and brought it somewhere near her mouth. The curly-haired girl grabbed Daniela's hand in support. Taking a big breath and then muttering a quick prayer, Daniela put the piece of steak in her mouth. Chewing twice, she swallowed hard.

"That's good steak, Joe," she managed to say. This Daniela girl had good manners!

Joe looked on proudly. "If you liked that, you'll love the sides I made. They're organic."

Gingerly, Daniela took a forkful of the stir fry.

"It smells like pop," said the guy beside her hopefully.

Daniela looked unconvinced. "I've, uh, never had beets and beans prepared this way before, Joe," she said trying not to grimace after sampling the stir fry. Without complaint and looking serious, Daniela scooped a forkful of the smelly gray mush.

"This one is the best. I pureed it myself," confided Joe.

The guy beside her looked very worried. "Daniela, this smells really funky. I mean it *all* smells funky but this smells like…"

He was too late. Maybe Daniela was just being nice or maybe she was trying to get the whole ordeal over with quickly so she could get back to her bagel. There was no way to know. But she downed the forkful of grey glop before her friend could finish his sentence.

And then she began to cough. The cough turned into a wheeze.

"Shellfish!" yelped the guy beside her whose name I soon found out was Adam. "Joe, what was in that puree?"

"Just mussels and leeks," said Joe.

Daniela's eyes began to water as she continued to cough.

"What's happening to Daniela?" asked Joe starting to panic. "Why is she getting red splotches all over her face and arms?"

"Those are hives, Joe—Daniela's allergic to shellfish," said Adam. "We need to take her to nurse right now!"

Joe no longer reminded me of my pup. He had turned into a protective bear. Scooping up wheezing Daniela, he threw her over his shoulder. "Follow me!" he shouted to Adam. "Don't worry, I've got you," he said to Daniela in a softer voice.

I had no idea where the nurse's office was but thankfully Joe did.

Chapter Twenty-Three

SUSPECT NUMBER ONE
☞ Andrea Hackenpack

The situation looked grim. I watched Joe throw Daniela over his shoulder like a sack of potatoes and bolt out of the cafeteria. Her friends Adam and Meena followed quickly behind.

"Someone needs to do something!" said Jenny in a panic as she grabbed my hand.

I had just gotten certified in advanced First Aid. CPR, burn treatments and tourniquets were all well within my wheelhouse. But my instructor barely touched on allergic reactions before moving on to sprained ankles. I did know that treatment for an acute allergic reaction was a shot of adrenaline and Daniela would be okay once she got a dose from her EpiPen.

Ms. Ahmed was our health teacher and the school nurse. In her office was a collection of pens for kids who were allergic to all sorts of things—from peanuts to eggs to soy to shellfish. Once Rocks Mudman tried to convince Ms. Ahmed he was allergic to math tests.

"But, Ms. Ahmed, I begin to sweat every time I have to take one! I start to hyperventilate and get pretty close to passing out," he told her. Ms. Ahmed just rolled her eyes.

Everyone in the cafeteria had seen (or smelled) the shellfish debacle. Some kids headed towards the nurse's station. Marlene was one of them.

"I think we should give them some space," I said to Jenny who nodded in agreement.

Marlene returned within a few minutes. "Joe sprinted all the way there," she said panting and out of breath describing the scene. "Ms. Ahmed gave Daniela a shot and then sent her home for the rest of the day. She'll be totally fine."

Poor Joe was another story. I saw him at his locker after school. He was a wreck. His friends were trying to cheer him up but it looked like someone had run over his dog or, in Joe's case, punctured his favourite basketball. I wanted to cheer him up —maybe by offering him some helpful advice on how to woo a Wilcott girl. His current advisor was totally off-base. Chocolates and flowers were a much better idea than steak with Cheez Whiz on it. I debated going up to him, giving him a hug and offering words of female wisdom. His head hung low as

Anil talked quietly in his ear. Joe nodded here and there but his shoulders never stopped stooping. Now didn't seem like the best time.

Chapter Twenty-four

SUSPECT NUMBER THREE
☞ Joe Jacobs

"Definitely not as bad as when I bent over to tie my cleats and ripped my football pants. That was in front of the whole school! Everyone could see my lucky Spidey undies!"

"Good thing you weren't wearing tighty whities that day!"

"Only thing worse than that was when I promised Stephanie Serrano I would hit a home run for her and I whiffed on three pitches instead."

"I remember that," said my mom. "You swung so hard at the last one that the bat hit you in the head. Then you walked to the wrong dugout and sat on the rival manager's lap."

"Coach LaRue!" laughed Marcus at the memory. "We still exchange Christmas cards."

"Definitely not as bad as when you misspelled your own name

on your spelling test," my dad added. "I still can't understand how you could spell *anatomically* correctly but not *Marcus*!"

"Remember that, Joe? Mr. Kagan called me *Mucus Jarcobs* for the rest of the year," said Marcus frowning.

"I remember that!" howled Mario. "It's one thing to get one letter wrong in your name. Everyone's done that. But two, bro? Classic!"

My family was doing their best to make me feel better. Mario had even given me his old phone, now that he had a new one.

"Now you can check the score whenever you like, little bro!"

But all the baseball scores in the world couldn't cheer me up—not after I had poisoned the girl of my dreams with shellfish puree.

Mario changed game plans. "You could say sorry with pizza. Classic margherita—just cheese and tomato sauce."

My mom agreed. "Something simple this time."

"Maybe spell out *I'm really sorry* in licorice," suggested Marcus.

"You could dot the '*i*'s in something special like chocolate-covered cherries," suggested my dad.

"We need to triple check that she doesn't have any fruit allergies," said Mario.

They were going into triple-overtime trying to make me feel better.

Sorry Spaghetti! Apology apple pie! Forgive me fruit roll-ups! Suggestions were flying back and forth faster than a 100 metres final.

"Maybe," I finally mumbled just to quiet them down. I wasn't sure how to fix this muddled up mussel mess but right now I just needed a time-out.

Chapter Twenty-five

SUSPECT NUMBER TWO
☞ Ralph Dorph

Joe Jacobs was the talk of the Dorph dinner table that night.

"The poor boy," said my mom after I told her about Joe's culinary catastrophe.

"I can sympathize," said my dad. "I brought your mom a bouquet of hydrangeas on our first date without realizing she suffers from intense hay fever."

Mom nodded and smiled, "And I forgave you, just like Daniela will eventually forgive Joe."

"I dunno, Mom," I said doubtfully, "she was really covered in red splotches. You had to see it to believe it. I don't even know Joe but I really felt bad for him."

"Well," said Mara, "on Monday you'll do Joe a favour by taking the spotlight off of him. Operation *Presents and Tees* is ready to go. No one will be talking about poor Joe Jacobs and his shellfish debacle when the day is over. They'll all be talking about the awesome Ralph Dorph!"

We had combed through Mara's closet and come up with some good ways to show off my *presents*. Combined with a trip to the local second hand store where we found old t-shirts for pennies, a Bedazzler, a glue gun and some tie dye, we made a bunch of different tees. For the basketball team there were tees with sweatbands attached (a little glue and string went a long way). The AV club got cool 3D tees. We made tees with tie dyed handkerchiefs for kids with colds and blue tees for kids feeling a bit depressed about the upcoming spelling test. In a stroke of genius—my sister's —we used my gigantic selection of turtlenecks to create cool tees for the chess club.

"I never ever want to see one of these again!" said Mara as she took a pair of scissors and hacked the long neck off of my favourite plaid shirt. She took the sad looking material, added some metallic studs and then resewed it onto the front.

"Try this on," she demanded. "I want to make sure it can bear weight."

I slipped on the tee. The studded material made a little pocket over my heart. Mara added a little shiny liner and then slipped three pens in between the materials.

"Now this is a pocket protector!" she said nodding at her

handiwork. "See, Ralphie, it is possible to be nerdy and stylish."

My sister sewed a tiny *RD* and a smiley face onto the bottom of each shirt. "Hard to notice at first but special once you do," she explained "just like you."

We boxed up the t-shirts carefully so they wouldn't wrinkle. "So I guess that makes us done," I said smiling. I had a good feeling about our *presents and tees* project. This time, Bossypants's advice was spot on.

I arrived early to school on Monday and immediately unpacked the tees. I had spent the last few days scoping out the various teams and clubs at school so I knew exactly when and where to find them. The basketball team was holding practice right now so I headed straight to the gym. The team was sitting on the floor watching Coach Carron as he wrote x's and o's on a chalkboard. He stopped talking as I approached.

I cleared my throat. "Hi." My confidence level had dipped a bit but it was still higher than when I stood on a table and invited everyone to hang at the wharf with Dorph. The team waited for me to continue. "I just need a minute of your time. I'm new here. My name is Ralph. Some of you might have heard of me. Or maybe you haven't heard of me... which might be a good thing after my Wild Wordy mess."

I heard few good-natured chuckles.

"Hopefully I'll get the chance to get to know you guys better.

There's a lot more to me than rhyming stanzas—now mandatory rhyming stanzas." More chuckling. This humour thing was working! I had established my *presents* and now it was time for the *tees*. "Just so I can show my support, I made some t-shirts for the team. I've got a bunch of mediums and larges and a few extra larges."

I started to hand them out. The guys looks surprised—kind of like Daniela when Joe placed the tray of food in front of her. But they relaxed when they saw the red tees. No smelly fish in sight! One guy—I think his name was Anil—slipped the shirt over his jersey.

"Cool," he said. "A built-in sweatband. This'll come in handy during our two minute drills."

I quickly summed up my little speech. "Hopefully you'll like them and think of Ralph Dorph when you wear them." I thought the last bit might have been overkill but I was caught up in the moment. The guys were smiling and, taking Anil's lead, putting on their new tees.

"Thanks for the support, Ralph," said Anil. "And I think I can speak for the team when I promise you'll have *our* support next week."

The rest of the team nodded. I wasn't sure what next week was—maybe there was a school dance and they knew how shy I was around girls or maybe it was about the upcoming history test. Regardless, support sounded good. I nodded enthusiastically. Even though I didn't know much about sports, eating lunch with the basketball team could be fun.

Before I left I scanned the room for Joe Jacobs. I couldn't find him. Maybe he had convinced his mom he needed a sick day? That would have been my tactic. I gave Anil an extra large shirt for Joe.

"Please make sure he gets it," I said to a nodding Anil. I'd introduce myself to Joe another day.

Chapter Twenty-six

SUSPECT NUMBER ONE
☞ Andrea Hackenpack

I was just toweling off from a tough 400 meter individual medley—finishing with the fastest freestyle split I had ever posted—when Ralph Dorph walked onto the pool deck. I didn't know Ralph well—except that he had raw talent as a poet—but, at first glance, he didn't strike me as the swim team type.

Lifting my goggles, I gave him a quick up and down: yes, he was incredibly skinny but he seemed to have a relatively long torso. His legs were short but his hands were rather large for his slight frame. Based on his oversized hands, I hypothesized that he most likely had large flipper-like feet. He was perfectly proportioned for swimming! Perhaps my initial assessment was off base and, with a bit of coaching, he would make a good butterflier. The boys' individual medley relay lacked a solid butterflier. I was about to approach Ralph and see if he was interested when, out of the blue, he started handing out t-shirts to my teammates.

"Cool," said Jenny as she put one of the tees on over her wet bathing suit.

"Ralph, this is awesome," said Ed Nojna as he held up a futuristic-looking garment. The shirt itself was plain but it came equipped with gigantic, rubberized shoulder pads that were fastened upside down. They looked like little pools. "How did you come up with the idea?"

Ralph explained, "Hannah Bennett—"

"That's me!" shouted Hannah as she climbed up the diving board. Her thick, long black hair flew in different directions as she somersaulted off the board. Quickly she breast-stroked towards us and hopped out of the pool.

"What's up, Ralph?" Her wet hair dripped all over Ralph's tennis shoes.

"Hannah Bennett sits in front of me in history class," tried Ralph again. "She comes sopping wet to class every Monday, Wednesday and Friday morning. Usually her hair drips all over my notebook and I when I go home after school and try to study, I can't read my notes because everything is waterlogged and blurry."

"Ralph, you should have told me!" said Hannah frowning.

"I can put my hair in a bun. It might not stop all the dripping, but it will help. Or you should have asked to borrow my notes!"

"That's okay. Rewriting all of my history notes seems to have helped me remember Ms. Pemberley's lectures. I got a B plus on last week's quiz on the War of 1812," said Ralph smiling.

"Your dripping hair also helped me come up with this great tee idea—a swimmer's tee. Me and my sister made shoulder pads out of some old rubber tires. Using hammers, we designed pads that would collect the drippy hair water."

Hannah admired her shirt. "I love the way the shoulder pads shimmer! I've got a pair of sandals that will look so good with this." She shook her wet hair. Droplets of chlorine-tinged water pooled in the shoulder pads instead of on Ralph's shoes. "It's fantastic, Ralph," summed up Hannah.

"Why did you come up with this idea?" I asked cautiously.

"Well, I'm new here," said Ralph, "and I'm not a great swimmer but this was a way to show my support to Wilcotters."

"Great shirt! Great idea," enthused Ed. "Now I won't catch a chill in homeroom."

"You've got my support," I heard him say quietly. Hannah and a few other kids nodded.

Concerned, Jenny looked at me. Evidently, Ralph Dorph was running for school president! I wasn't sure what to say. His campaign, *"Show My Support to Wilcotters"* via t-shirts was ingenious—much more effective than my Bossypants campaign was proving to be. Practice had finished, so I quickly changed out of my swimsuit and made a beeline for my locker. Ralph seemed like a nice guy but he hadn't attended any of the candidate meetings. Although I wasn't afraid of a little competition, I was positive Ralph missed the deadline for declaring his candidacy. In fact, I was pretty sure he was going to school in Paris or Japan when the nomination forms needed to filled out. He didn't know a thing about Wilcott student council. It was a shame because his witty campaign made me think he would have been a solid choice for vice president.

I opened my locker and grabbed my student body handbook and flipped to page 56—the page that outlined Wilcott's student council bylaws. I was right! Ralph was not eligible to be president as it was too late to sign up. Furthermore, I doubted that he had secured the signatures of twenty fellow Wilcotters to support his nomination. I set off to gently break the news to Ralph. On the bright side, he could be class rep next year. And I was pretty positive he had a bright future swimming butterfly.

I found Ralph near the cafeteria handing out more t-shirts. Gone were the funky swimming tees. And the cool shirts I saw the basketball team wearing earlier were nowhere in sight. This time, Ralph was giving out peculiar, downright ugly shirts. The colour palette was muddy brown and grimy green and they smelled dank like a pair of sandals you peel off your sticky feet on a hot day. Looking closer, I noticed bits of slime hanging off the shirts. It appeared to be overcooked pasta sewed together in random patterns. Green peas were caked around the collars. My fellow Wilcotters were avoiding Ralph and his grungy shirts.

Curiosity got the best of me and overpowered my sense of smell. "What kind of tees are these?" I asked, forgetting the bad news I'd planned on breaking to him.

"I made them out of last night's dinner," said Ralph. I must have looked confused because he added, "I know they're a bit gross but sometimes you have to *make yourself noticed and disgust.*"

His words caught my attention; that was my catchphrase. Well, normally it was. It's good to put yourself out there—but not this time. I grabbed a t-shirt to be polite and then headed off. My free time was extra valuable today. The vital first round of presidential speeches was at the end of the week! I'd finally get a chance to see what the other candidates brought to the table—surely Marty had more than meatballs to offer— and my classmates would get a first-hand chance to see what made Andrea Hackenpack special. I wrote my speech last month and had it memorized cold, but I needed to make a few last minute tweaks. I had a lot to do today! It wasn't until bedtime that I realized I had forgotten to break the bad news about the election to Ralph.

Chapter Twenty-seven

SUSPECT NUMBER TWO
☞ Ralph Dorph

It took almost a week to hand out all of the shirts. All in all, I was satisfied with my *presents and tees* campaign. I gave my family a detailed recap over dinner. "Everyone really liked their shirts. Hannah wore hers in history class, and for the first time ever, I don't have to recopy any soggy notes. A swimmer named Ed seems pretty nice. And a group called Wilcotters for the Ethical Treatment of Poor Defenceless Animals loved my *disgusting* tees. They're aiming to go green this year and think shirts made out of compost and leftover dinner could be the next big thing."

"Pretty much everyone I met this week promised to support me," I told them. "Kind of weird words to use, but I'll take it."

"Well, I think it's sweet," said my mom. "They must know what it's like to be the new kid in town. Just be sure to wear clean underwear tomorrow because you are going to have a zillion friends fighting over you."

Mara looked at me and rolled her eyes. I had no idea what clean underwear had to do with things, but, hopefully my mom was right about the zillion friends. Creating all the tees with Mara was fun, but it was worthless if I ended up lunching alone yet again.

The next morning, I put on one of my favourite new tees and headed to school. Enthusiasm over my t-shirt campaign still seemed to be in the air. A bunch of kids I had never met before slapped me on the back and smiled. A few girls even wished me luck. My worries about the third period math quiz must have been obvious.

"See you in the cafeteria, Ralph," said Hannah as we left history.

"Catch you in the caf, Ralph!" yelled Anil from across the hall.

Lunchtime was looking good!

"Don't be nervous!" added his friend Jonah Isaacs. "Meatball Marty's no competition."

I had no idea what he was talking about. While my new popularity was a bit overwhelming, I wouldn't go so far to say it made me nervous. And I had no idea what a meatball marty was, though I was willing to try one for lunch.

The first thing I noticed when I entered the cafeteria was

the noise—it was buzzing with loud chatter. The second thing I noticed was the podium which had been set up along the north wall. Two chairs apiece sat on each side of the platform.

"Ralph! Great to see you!" said Mr. Kagan, grabbing my arm and steering me towards the empty chairs. "I loved your *presents and tees* campaign."

He lowered his voice. "I want to apologize about Wild Wordy Wednesday. I didn't realize it would backfire and the kids would blame you. Your campaign has completely wiped the wordy brouhaha away. I really think you have a shot at this."

I was trying to figure out what he was talking about as he ushered me into one of the empty seats to the left of the podium.

"Best of luck with your speech, Ralph," said Mr. Kagan clasping me on the shoulder. "Nail it and you'll give yourself a solid shot to become the next president of J.R. Wilcott."

For a split second time seemed to freeze, giving me the chance to catch up. Suddenly everything made sense. Kids were wearing my tees and promising to support me—and my presidential campaign! Hannah, Anil, Ed and the rest of school thought I was trying to become their next leader. I looked down at my monogrammed RD t-shirt. Ugh! Now I could see how everyone thought I was in the presidential race. I didn't have much time to come up with a plan. A wispy girl with glasses sat down beside me and introduced herself as Gwenn Yoon. On the other side of the podium, an outspoken girl named Andrea Hackenpack took a seat. The last chair was quickly filled by a guy shovelling the last bite of a cheeseburger in his mouth— Meatball Marty, I assumed.

Mr. Kagan stepped up to the podium and made a long speech that I didn't really hear. I was too busy trying to figure out what my next move, or really my only move, was. Should I just go for it and ad lib a speech? Should I explain that my *presents and tees* campaign wasn't really that kind of *campaign*? Or should I just bolt out of the cafeteria without saying a word? None of my choices seemed like a winner. I wasn't interested in being class president; I'd look lame explaining the logic behind the shirts; and I'd cement my reputation as an all-out nerd if I ran out of the cafeteria right now. All I wanted was to have some company as I ate my lunch! I wasn't paying attention to Mr. Kagan until I heard my name.

"I am proud to introduce our first candidate," he started. "He's attended several middle schools around the world so, if elected, he can bring an international flavour to our student council. Let's all give a hand to Ralph Dorph."

Mr. Kagan gestured to me and stepped away from the podium. Ready or not, like it or not, I was running for school president! Slowly I stepped up to the podium. Never giving much thought to school politics, I had no idea what went in a wannabe president's speech. Plus I had a big disadvantage. Being new to school, I didn't know much about Wilcott's history. Taking a walk down J.R. Wilcott's memory lane was out of the question. Having never served on Wilcott's student council, I couldn't brag about years of experience and expertise. My only option was to promise everyone I'd improve school. Problem was, I wasn't exactly sure what needed to be improved. I'd have to be thorough and cover all of my bases.

"If elected, I promise to make the cafeteria food better," I started. "The beef stroganoff is pretty bad so I'll try and get it changed to something better."

"Like mac n' cheese?" called out someone from the audience.

"Sure, like mac n' cheese." I confirmed. The audience applauded so I continued.

"If elected..." I paused and looked around the room, zoning in on the half-empty vending machine, "I'll make sure the vending machine is always stocked with chips."

It was a weak promise but a voice popped up from the crowd, "And Cheezies?"

"And Cheezies," I confirmed. More applause. So far so good! I gained steam as I continued.

"If elected, I promise to add a school dance at the end of the year." I had no idea if J.R. Wilcott held any dances but the crowd nodded in approval. "I promise to make sure teachers don't mark in red ink. I promise to get extra padding for the chairs in the library so we don't get sore as we study and I promise to eliminate any pop quizzes popped on a Friday."

Wilcotters cheered in approval.

"I promise to make sure the caretakers supply us with better toilet paper—at least three ply, I promise to replace *Romeo and Juliet* with *Spiderman*, I promise to have the water fountains changed to Coca-Cola fountains, I promise to have a field trip to the mall and finally, I promise to outlaw all grades under a B minus if you elect Ralph Dorph!" I pumped both hands in the air as an exclamation mark and Wilcotters of all ages stood up and cheered. I had nothing left to promise. Exhausted, I sat down.

Chapter Twenty-eight

SUSPECT NUMBER THREE
☞ Joe Jacobs

Ralph Dorph was on fire! His speech was the first thing to cheer me up in days. Cheezies, chips, Spiderman and no more pop quizzes ruining a perfectly good Friday—this was the best thing I'd heard in awhile. If Ralph had been giving me advice, I never would have poisoned the girl I wanted to take out.

Mario had driven me over to Daniela's house that night so I could apologize in person. And she was pretty cool about it— forgave me on the spot. But I still felt lousy about the whole deal. But Ralph Dorph's promise to change all the water fountains to Coca-Cola fountains made my day a bit better. In my opinion, Ralph's speech was an uncontested layup.

Andrea Hackenpack was up next. She was very smart and sure to offer up some solid suggestions. But, before she could go for it, Marty Jenkins insisted on having a private talk with Mr. Kagan. He looked surly—although not as furious as I'd seen him earlier. I'd run into Marty on my way to the cafeteria. He had Harold Wormald cornered and was waving his arms in the air. At first I thought he was showing Harold how to defend a jump shot but, as I got closer, I heard his voice. He wasn't yelling but I could tell he was mad. I had no idea what had him so riled up but he kept repeating, "This wasn't the plan!" It kind of summed up the way I felt about my steak dinner. I couldn't hear Harold's reply but I could tell he was working hard to calm Marty down.

Now Marty was talking seriously to Mr. Kagan. I thought about using this little break to introduce myself to Ralph Dorph. He had given Anil a cool tee for me and I wanted to thank him. Ralph and I had never actually met so it was amazing he knew what a sweater I was—the built-in sweatband was a whole new level of awesome! I was about to head over when Mr. Kagan motioned for Ralph to join their discussion. Soon Andrea and Gwenn Yoon were also in the scrum. After a lot of head nodding, the huddle broke and Mr. Kagan went to the podium.

"I'd like to thank Ralph Dorph for giving such an inspired speech," he said. Maybe he liked Ralph's speech so much that it was a forfeit? President Ralph, Coca Cola and comic books were here to stay! "But it has just been called to my attention that Ralph's candidacy violates the J.R. Wilcott bylaws which states that all candidates have to be nominated by a fellow student and have twenty other students support the nomination via signature. I am sorry to announce that Ralph Dorph cannot run for school president. But I thank him for giving us many helpful suggestions on how to improve the school."

"Is it too late to nominate him now?" I called out from the back of the room. "I'll do it."

"It's way too late, Jacobs," answered Marty instantly. "Way too late. Nominations had to be completed last month. Try again next year."

Mr. Kagan told Ralph he could remain on the podium but Ralph excused himself instead. Even though his dream of running J.R. Wilcott was crushed, he didn't look all that disappointed. Andrea finally took the stand and began to speak. I made a quick break for Ralph. Bobbing and weaving through some grade sixes and sevens, I was right behind him when I got intercepted by the Principal Losman. He probably wanted to talk to me about the whole 'making the girl you like break out in hives' mess. Or maybe he wanted to remind me I missed a history test when my mom let me stay home from school. I was pretty sure I could talk my way out of that one. Principal Losman was all right. I'm sure he'd get how embarrassing it was to poison a girl in front of the whole school. As I began explaining myself, he gently pushed me aside. It wasn't me Principal Losman was after. It was Ralph Dorph!

"You really hit the nail on the Wilcott head with that speech, Ralph. I'm not sure it's sensible to replace our water fountains with Coke, but many of your other suggestions can be tinkered with and implemented. We might not replace Shakespeare with Spiderman, but there's no reason why we can't expand the graphic novels section in the library."

Ralph smiled and nodded but didn't say anything. He looked unsure of what to expect from Principal Losman. I had a feeling: duck for cover, Ralph!

"I'm sorry you can't run for president but unfortunately it's impossible to change the rules at this late date. On the other hand, Ralph, it would be a shame to lose an innovative voice like yours," continued the principal.

Ralph was still smiling but his lips started to twitch. My mouth did that too when I was nervous.

"So I've come up with what I think is a win-win solution."

Here it comes!

"You and I head up a think tank!"

Bam!

"I propose that we meet after school every Monday and Friday until the end of the school year. We can work on some of your campaign suggestions and we can also put our heads together and come up with other ways to improve Wilcott."

Ralph remained silent but the twitching was getting worse.

"What do you think, Ralph? I really think you and I can work together and make a great team."

This was brutal! Principal Losman was okay but I'm pretty sure there were a million other teams Ralph wanted to be on.

Ralph finally spoke. "I think it's a good idea, Principal Losman, but I'm not sure I can stay after school every Monday and Friday. Those are the days I have to walk my dog. My dad made a schedule and I need to get home right after school on those days to walk Pepper."

Total props to Ralph's skills. He was doing his best to get out of this mess, but keeping it totally polite. I'd try this tactic the next time my mom leaned on me to rake the leaves or take out the trash.

Principal Losman thought for a moment. He was determined to make this work. "How about at lunch time? We'll dine together every Tuesday and Thursday and toss around ideas as we eat our lunch. I'll sweeten the pot with dessert. Mrs. Losman is a great baker—I'll get her to provide us with a few sweets to make it worth your while!" He smiled and gave Ralph a pat on the shoulder to seal the deal.

Double whammy. There wasn't much Ralph could say, poor guy. He woke up this morning hoping to be school president and instead he was stuck eating lunch with the principal twice a week. Even if Mrs. L made a great chocolate cake, this stunk.

"Looking forward to our first power lunch!" called Principal Losman over his shoulder as he headed back to the speeches.

I thought about approaching Ralph. I had first hand experience with an awesome plan going completely haywire. But, Ralph's face was turning a strange colour—a crazy combination of green and red. Before I could go up to him, he bolted straight out of the cafeteria.

Chapter Twenty-nine

SUSPECT NUMBER TWO
☞ Ralph Dorph

Arrrrrgh! Even though I was sitting on the floor of my closet, in my locked room, in my house, with the windows closed, I was pretty sure the rest of the street could hear me screaming. I threw a cold, probably dirty, towel over my head and continued to yell. Still, I'm pretty sure they could hear me screaming.

I told my parents I'd come out of my room when I was ready. I couldn't talk about this just yet. A stupid think tank! A stupid, dumb think tank! As much as I liked fresh-baked goods, there was nothing good about this think tank. Sure, now I had company for lunch—if you count Principal Losman as company! All the *support* I had from the rest of the school was sure to be forgotten if I was caught nibbling on Mrs. Losman's carrot-ginger muffins. I wouldn't have a chance to get to know the other kids; I'd be too busy recommending flavours of chips for the vending machines. How things got worse than Wild Wordy Wednesday I had no idea, but somehow my reputation as Ralph Dorph, supernerd, got cemented. Was it worth it to write to Bossypants and tell her what a mess my life was now? There was no way I'd listen to any more of her crummy advice but maybe I could stop her from ruining another new kid's life. I wasn't sure of anything right now except that it felt good yelling my head off.

Thank goodness it was Friday and I had the weekend to sit in my closet and stew. I was already formulating a plan to get out of school next week, too. I was scheduled to visit the Ears, Nose and Throat clinic Monday morning. After the appointment I would convince my mom to let me take the rest of the day off. I'd come up with a plan for the rest of the week later. Until then, I planned on sitting in my closet.

Chapter Thirty

SUSPECT NUMBER ONE
☞ Andrea Hackenpack

Joe Jacobs and Ralph Dorph! It hit me right in between my appetizer and main course. Even though it was Sunday night, my parents had taken me out for a special dinner to celebrate all the hard work I had put into my campaign. Elections were tomorrow—I think they were trying to help me relax via molten chocolate cake.

I recounted my speech as I polished off my bruschetta. "I think I nailed it. Mr. Kagan said it was one of the most comprehensive campaign speeches in the history of J.R. Wilcott. I offered up a new vision for the school as I simultaneously incorporated touches from famous former Wilcott presidents. I truly think I showed my fellow Wilcotters what I can bring to the table as their new leader."

"What's next on the agenda?" asked my dad.

"We have one last chance tomorrow morning to plead our case—just a minute or two to make a final appeal to the student body. Then voting begins," I told him.

"Is this when you're going to reveal that you're the brains behind Bossypants?" inquired my mom.

I hadn't kept my parents up-to-date on my success as a peer advisor because there wasn't any success to speak of. My first round of advice went down like a ton of bricks. And, while no news can sometimes be good news, I wasn't sure that was the case with my second round of advice. There were no new couples strolling the halls and I hadn't noticed any new friendships spark up. Without any successes to point to, my big reveal as the brain behind the Bossypants app (™!) was pointless.

"I think I'm going to table Bossypants for the time being," I told them. "I've got so many other things going for me in this campaign that I don't think I need Bossypants to boost my profile."

Although I had been regularly adding more content to my app, I just wasn't getting the digital followers I had hoped for. I switched back to good old paper for my final push. Mr. Kagan had given me permission to bring the Grade Seven Gazette back to life for one special print run. Marlene and Jenny helped me produce an *All About Andrea* special edition. It included an exclusive interview with my kindergarten teacher, an in-depth interview with my grade five music teacher and an all-access/all inclusive/ no holds-barred interview with myself. There wasn't much more I could do to show Wilcott what made Andrea Hackenpack tick.

My dad nodded. "You've done great work over the past year, Andrea. Your last report card was full of A's and your extracurricular activities are extensive. You've worked diligently to get yourself noticed and discussed in all the right ways."

My last piece of bruschetta—the crusty end—suddenly lodged in my throat. *Get yourself noticed and discussed.* I finally realized who my two clients were—Ralph Dorph and Joe Jacobs! Oh no! I started to cough violently. The bread dislodged and dropped like a brick into my churning stomach. I took a sip of water but I still couldn't stop coughing.

"Did it go down the wrong pipe?" asked my mother as she patted me on the back.

I felt both flushed and chilled. My dad looked concerned when I brought my napkin to my mouth—there was a fifty percent chance I was going to throw up. I didn't know how my advice had backfired, but it most definitely had and with catastrophic consequences. Joe "New To Women" Jacobs sent the girl of his dreams into anaphylactic shock. And poor Ralph "New To Wilcott" Dorph was not only the Wild Wordy Wednesday scapegoat but, rumour had it, had been recruited to lunch with Principal Losman twice a week. It had been a horrendous month for Joe and Ralph because of me! I wasn't exactly sure how *"wow her with flowers"* led to a repulsive steak dinner. *"Leave a lasting impression"* could be more easily misinterpreted, though was a stretch to imagine Ralph wanting to charm Principal Losman into a lunch date. How could my advice have gotten so misinterpreted? Was there more wrong with the app? I quickly retrieved my phone and went to my sent mail, but the screen still wouldn't load. I'd have to call Harold about this again after dinner. Regardless, both disasters were on my shoulders.

I couldn't believe it took me so long to figure out that Joe and Ralph were N.T.W. and N.T.W. respectively. I desperately needed to make it up to them. I barely tasted my Fettuccini Alfredo as my mind went into overdrive. And the molten chocolate cake that followed could have been stale bread. I was too busy formulating a plan—a disaster relief plan—to notice anything else.

Neither Joe nor Ralph had asked for more advice—why would they at this point?—but I couldn't stay silent. They both needed the same words of wisdom: don't give up! I sent them both the same message.

> *Dear N.T.W.,*
>
> *I haven't heard back from you but I just want to say, don't give up! You are this close to achieving your goal. It can still be done! Be yourself, be open and be*

honest. Things are about to turn around and everything will work out. I believe in you!

I had given both cases a lot of thought. Although Joe had given Daniela hives, I still thought his dilemma was less complicated than Ralph's. I truly believed Joe still had a shot with Daniela. The steak dinner might have been off-the-charts gross but the idea behind it was sweet. Ralph's situation was more complex. It wasn't easy being the new guy in school. And it was even harder to make friends. While Wilcotters had finally forgiven Ralph for Wild Wordy Wednesday, from what I could see, he still hadn't made a special connection with anyone. I added a few extra lines in Ralph's email.

I have an idea that might appeal to you. Wilcott is offering a new intramural sport and it will be a great way to meet people. Have you heard of rounders? It's a lot like softball but you don't use a glove when you play the field. No equipment needed! A pitcher throws the ball to the batter. The batter hits the ball and runs the bases. Pretty simple and lots of excitement. Not only will it be fun but it will be a great way to make friends.

Hopefully this would finally put Ralph on the right path. The possibility of winning the school presidency tomorrow wasn't as exciting now that I knew I might have ruined Ralph's first year at J.R. Wilcott.

Chapter Thirty-one

SUSPECT NUMBER THREE
☞ Joe Jacobs

Election day reminds me of game day. Everyone's nervous and excited at the same time. The three candidates reminded me of boxers doing last minute prep before a big fight. Andrea was a heavyweight. She was in one corner of the cafeteria, reviewing her cue cards. Her trainer, Jenny Mitchell, massaged her shoulders. Gwenn Yoon was more like a featherweight. She was in the other corner taking some deep breathes. Gwenn was an underrated contender and had it in her to pull an upset. Jenkins, he was a classic counter puncher—scrappy and wily. I had just passed him in the hall. He had Wormald cornered yet again except this time they were laughing.

"Intramural rounders," said Harold.

I stopped when I heard the word *rounders* and turned

towards them. I loved rounders! It was all the fun of baseball without the annoyance of having to remember your glove. Since when did we have intramural rounders?

"Now she's suggesting he play *lunch menu rounders*!" said Harold giggling.

Marty started to crack up. "Brilliant! Your original idea of sending Andrea's advice to the wrong person was solid. We got that ridiculous Wild Wordy Wednesday out of it. But you really showed your game with the homophone gag. I didn't think it was possible to top *show her your mussels* but you totally did! Lunch menu rounders—I love it! You're a genius, Harold. An evil genius. I can only hope to continue your legacy next year when I'm president."

"I am good," sniffed Harold. "You should have asked me to be your campaign manager."

I had no idea what they were talking about but they looked really impressed with themselves. Marty needed to motor because the assembly was starting in five minutes.

I immediately spotted Daniela in the cafeteria. She was sitting in a corner reading. Now looked like a pretty good time to go and talk to her. I heard Anil call my name. He pointed to an empty seat beside him. I waved back to him and gave him the two minutes sign. I really wanted to say hi to Daniela. Aside from apologizing a thousand times as I carried her to the nurse and stopping by her house later that night to apologize again, I hadn't spoken to her since the steak incident. But Anil kept waving me over and Daniela never looked up from her book. It must have been a good one. I took one last glance at Daniela and then headed over to Anil.

Mr. Kagan kept his intro short today. We all knew the players. They were just taking their final at bats. Andrea went first. She quickly reminded us why Wilcott was a good school and how she could make it even better. Andrea was a natural at this kind of stuff. She reminded me of Mario playing tennis. He serves ace after ace after ace without the help of any lessons. He just has it. And so does Andrea. Up next was Jenkins. If Andrea reminded me of Mario, Jenkins was more like Marcus. Marcus was the most competitive person I knew. Last summer he practiced for two hours every night just so he could tell us at dinner how he had beaten Mario in a fifth set tie-breaker. Both Jenkins and Marcus were in it to win it.

Jenkins took the stage and cleared his throat. He started off a lot like Andrea, telling us how he could make Wilcott a better place. Suddenly, he pulled a U-turn.

"I've told you what I can do for Wilcott," he told us seriously, "but I haven't told you what my opponent"—he stopped and pointed to a startled looking Andrea—"*did* for Wilcott."

"Who here remembers Wild Wordy Wednesday?" asked Marty. A few kids started to boo. A couple others started to hiss. "It was all her!" said Marty loudly. "She masterminded the whole thing!"

Andrea's mouth fell open in shock. Marty Jenkins continued.

"Andrea Hackenpack is the so-called brains behind the Bossypants app (™!). Anyone who used her app—and there weren't many—regretted it. Her advice was brutal! Do you really want someone running Wilcott who suggested the new guy makes friends via weekly poetry assignments? Does a real leader convince a male student to poison a female student via rotten fishy steak? Someone he wanted to impress and go out with, might I add. I won't get into specifics but, trust me, Andrea's so-called words of wisdom are not to be trusted."

As Marty took a breath, the whole room turned to Andrea, waiting for her to fight back and take down Jenkins. She opened her mouth to defend herself, but, probably for the first time ever, no words came out. She wasn't frowning, smiling or crying. Her face was blank. Her expression reminded me of when Wilcott lost the basketball final to McKelvin by 45 points. 'Shell-shocked' was the expression my mom used to describe the feeling.

I had figured out Daniela wasn't Bossypants around the time she broke into hives and I had to carry her to the nurse's office. Even if it was Andrea who screwed up my chances with

Daniela, I didn't like the way this fight was going down.

"It's a dirty fight," I whispered to Anil. "Come on, Andrea, get up off the canvas and defend yourself."

But Andrea just sat there speechless as Marty continued. "Andrea Hackenpack wants to lead Wilcott but we can't let her. She'll do what she thinks is best for the school and suddenly we'll be having poetry slams twice a week...maybe even three times. The cafeteria will start serving rancid mussel puree every Thursday!"

Jenkins was punching below the belt. My puree wasn't that bad! And Andrea wasn't a bad person. I stopped writing to Bossypants when I realized Daniela wasn't behind the app. But, late last night, my phone pinged. There was a message from Bossypants telling me not to give up. Andrea's advice might not have been perfect but at least she was trying.

Marty attempted to put the nail in Andrea's presidential coffin. "If Andrea Hackenpack is in charge of your school, any *good* idea you have will get twisted into a *terrible* idea. A vote for Marty Jenkins is a vote for *your* Wilcott!"

Marty finally sat down. He looked incredibly impressed with himself. Andrea sat beside him, her head hung low in shame. The rest of the room exploded! Everyone had something to say. Some kids ran up to Marty to get the juicy details. A few kids tried to make Andrea feel better. Most started gossiping with the person beside them. I used the time out to put it all together. Andrea was Bossypants. I used her app. According to Marty Jenkins, Ralph Dorph also used her app. He was the *new guy* trying to make friends. I looked around for Ralph but he was nowhere to be seen. Daniela was also missing.

"Are you okay?" asked Anil.

"Yeah, why?" I asked him confused. Andrea was the one in trouble, not me.

"Because Marty Jenkins just told the whole school you like Daniela Olafson," said Anil.

Good point! A few grade sixes were looking at me and pointing. But Jacobs bros have thick skin. On the scale of humiliation, all of Wilcott knowing I liked Daniela ranked pretty low. It wasn't like I had missed a shot at the buzzer or anything. Most of my friends had already figured it out anyway. Mr. Kagan tried to restore order but it was impossible. I could hear kids talking about Ralph. I could hear kids talking about Andrea.

"Mr. Papernick asked her for advice on next week's algebra test and she told him to eliminate all bonus marks!" said someone.

"I heard she told him to ban all make-up tests," remarked someone else.

"I heard that Ralph, Andrea and Joe are going to have dinner at Principal Losman's tomorrow night and that Mrs. Losman baked a special chocolate cake in the shape of J.R. Wilcott. The first floor is vanilla and the second floor is chocolate and the gymnasium is filled with coconut cream," a girl in grade six told her friends.

I loved anything with coconut cream in it! Unfortunately, the girl was wrong. True or not, all of Wilcott had something to say about the scandal. Poor Gwenn Yoon never got a chance to deliver her speech.

Chapter Thirty-two

SUSPECT NUMBER TWO
☞ Ralph Dorph

If I had thought lunching with Principal Losman was rock bottom, I was wrong. The Ears, Nose and Throat doctor wanted to run some extra tests on me. Ugh.

"Today's your lucky day, Ralph. The appointment after you cancelled so I have enough time to check both of your nasal cavities and your inner ear drums."

I was positive I'd hit rock bottom as I tilted my head backwards so she could insert a thin tube up my nose. It was almost lunchtime by the time my mom and I were back in the car.

"So...it's almost noon and I'm beat. I should probably just spend the afternoon resting on the couch," I tried.

"You still have half a day of school left," said my mother shaking her head.

"I've already missed the most important subjects of the day. I've just got gym and geography left." I wasn't giving up. I did not want to show my face at school today. "Plus the doctor said I need to take it easy. I'm pretty sure we're wrestling in gym today."

My mom wasn't giving in. "You're going to school, Ralph." She pulled out of the parking lot and headed towards Wilcott. "I thought you said today was the big election. Don't you want to vote?"

"Not really," I mumbled. And it was true. I didn't know any of the candidates very well.

"It's your civic duty to vote," said my mother.

I tuned her out by pulling out my phone. It had pinged late last night due to a mail from Bossypants. I hadn't written to her since the think-tank mess. And with good reason—she had ruined my Wilcott social life! Like usual, her advice made no sense.

Dear N.T.W.,

I haven't heard back from you yet but I just want to tell you, don't give up! You are this close to achieving your goal. It can still be done! Be yourself, be open and be honest. Things are about to turn around and everything will work out. I believe in you!

I have an idea that might appeal to you. Wilcott is offering a new intramural sport. Have you heard of Secret **Lunch Menu** *Rounders? It's a lot like softball but you* *don't use a glove when you play the* **meatloaf.** *No freshly* **squeezed orange juice** *needed. A pitcher throws the* **mashed potatoes** *to the batter. The batter hits the* **green beans and carrots** *and runs the bases. Pretty* **Organic** *and lots of* **apple pie** *excitement. Not only will it be fun but it will be a great way to make friends! Keep your eyes and ears open for the secret sign that the game has started!*

Shaker Heights Middle School had a rounders team so I knew it was pretty much like baseball but without the glove. But I had no idea what Secret Lunch Menu rounders was. It was easy to figure out why it was secret because no teacher would ever approve of it. Play the meatloaf? Throw the mashed potatoes to the batter? Hit the green beans and carrots? It was ridiculous nonsense. I was finished with Bossypants and her lunatic advice. I reread her message as my mom drove me to school and deleted it as we pulled up to the front door.

"Have a good afternoon," said my mom giving me a quick kiss. "And don't forget to vote!"

Chapter Thirty-three

SUSPECT NUMBER ONE
☞ Andrea Hackenpack

I needed to find Ralph Dorph and Joe Jacobs to apologize! Now that the secret was out, the veil of anonymity went with it. Marty's attack took me by surprise. It was a low blow to both my campaign and my reputation. I regrouped after a pep talk from Jenny and began to put the pieces of the puzzle together. Although Marty had been working on toppling me since Kindergarten, there was no way he had figured out my secret identity on his own. Someone had tipped him off. And, aside from Jenny, there was only one person at school who knew I was Bossypants. I found Harold right after the wretched assembly and looked him straight in the eye. He looked down at the floor confirming my suspicions.

"Double-crossing jerk!" I muttered to myself as I walked away. I'd deal with him later.

"Marty is a total sleaze," agreed Jenny as she walked beside me. I didn't bother to correct her. They were both sleazy.

"I wonder how long he was planning to out you as Bossypants," mused Jenny. "I bet he had it planned from the beginning."

Jenny was several steps behind me in assembling the puzzle and was murky on the details. She knew nothing about Harold's involvement. But something she said made a light bulb go off in my head. This was planned all along!

"I can't believe he sabotaged me like this," I shouted angrily.

"Marty Jenkins will do anything to win, especially against you. Ever since Bubbles the goldfish," said Jenny. "I really hope no one votes for him even if he promised May to be all-you-can-eat meatball month."

Marty's dumb promises were not on my revenge-horizon right now. I was still fixated on Harold. More pieces started to fit together. Not only did he sell me out to Marty, but he must have been tampering with the Bossypants app (™!) since the beginning. I wasn't sure what he did, but I was 99 percent sure *he* was behind the mangled advice. Somehow, he had convinced Ralph Dorph to stand up on a table and recite a poem. Somehow, he had convinced Joe Jacobs to woo Daniela with a stinky, Cheez Whiz steak. The technical details were fuzzy but I knew Harold had been behind the whole thing since the start.

As I made my way down the hall with Jenny, Joe Jacobs was

suddenly standing in front of me.

"Are you okay, Andrea?" he asked.

"Joe, I'm so sorry about what happened with Daniela!"

"It's okay. I got your little pep talk yesterday and I know you meant well."

"Joe, can I look at your phone for a second? I need to see the emails I sent you via the app. I think Harold and Marty had something to do with this gigantic mess."

"Harold?" asked Jenny.

"Yeah, he helped me create the app."

Joe quickly got out his phone and tapped on the app. "Check it out," he said as he handed over his phone.

My suspicions were instantly confirmed as I scanned the messages I had sent to him. They were totally different from what I had originally written and *thought* I'd sent.

"Ugh, I knew it!" I flashed the screen at Jenny. "Harold turned all my sweet suggestions into atrocious advice." I stopped cold and grabbed Jenny's hand. "Oh no! I sent Ralph advice last night. It was pretty detailed. Who knows what Harold did to it! I need to find Ralph Dorph before it's too late!"

Chapter Thirty-four

SUSPECT NUMBER TWO
☞ Ralph Dorph

I headed straight to the cafeteria hoping to have enough time to eat before the bell rang. Wilcott teachers were usually pretty strict about kids hanging out in the halls during lunch but today the halls were filled with grade sixes, sevens and eights. Everyone was talking a mile a minute. I could hear shouting coming from the cafeteria with the names *Marty* and *Andrea* repeated again and again. Looks like I had missed some pretty exciting final speeches!

As I stood in line to get some mashed potatoes I was overcome with the feeling that everyone was staring at me and whispering. But the cafeteria was so loud I could only catch a word here or there. It would have been nice to have someone to talk to about it but no one waved me over. I went to sit by myself again.

Today's lunch wasn't very appetizing. The meatloaf looked dry; the mashed potatoes were lumpy; and over-cooked green beans were my least favourite vegetable. Normally, I loved a good glass of orange juice, but Wilcott's OJ was full of icky, throat-tickling pulp. Apple Pie was the only edible looking thing on my plate. The unappetizing meal reminded me of Bossypants's last mail. Like usual, it was nonsense. *Secret lunch menu rounders?* Huh? *Play the meatloaf.* Ridiculous! *A pitcher throws mashed potatoes to the batter.* How does one even do that? I didn't have extensive experience in the food fight department—dinner at the Dorph house was rather tame—and I had no idea how mashed potatoes could be thrown like a baseball. They'd explode in the air as they travelled to home plate!

"*Battered*. She was totally battered up there," I heard some guy say.

"I know! And right after her *pitch*. But Dorph definitely had them all out-pitched," his friend replied.

The words batter and pitch made me stop. Secret Lunch Menu Rounders could *not* be real. Was I supposed to be the pitcher? Who was the batter? This was nuts! As crazy as it seemed, I kept hearing more clues.

"They picked a pretty hard *play* this year."

"Yeah, it's harder than this *meatloaf*!"

"That's one full *plate* you've got there."

Was that home plate? What play was I supposed to go for? If they wanted me to play this game, I should at least look like I made an effort. I started with a small spoonful of mashed potatoes. I'd have to pack it tightly if it was going to travel very far. I added another spoonful, creating a small but firm ball. Physics class didn't start until next year but common sense told me the mashed potato ball needed to be weighted equally if it was going to make it to home plate.

"I wish he'd *throw* me a bone," someone from the table next to me said.

"You should ask Hannah. They're on a first-name *basis*." I heard his friend say.

Throw? Bases? Hannah's on first base? The more I heard, the more Secret Lunch Menu Rounders started to sound real. J.R Wilcott was turning out to be one of the craziest schools I had attended.

Using my bare hands, I packed each spoonful tightly. When I finished I had a ball of potato about the same size as a softball.

"I heard Anil wants to take a *swing* at it," another one of the guys said.

"Hope he *goes for it*," said the other.

I looked over at Anil's table. He stood there, talking with the rest of the jocks, waving a foam sword from last week's drama rehearsal. He looked in my direction and gave a thumbs up. So,

Anil was at bat and I was the pitcher! This was it—the call of Secret Lunch Menu Rounders. I let loose.

It turns out mashed potatoes can travel clear across the cafeteria.

Chapter Thirty-five

SUSPECT NUMBER ONE
☞ Andrea Hackenpack

After a quick pass through the halls, I circled back to the cafeteria to search for Ralph. There, I ran into Harold again. I had to know why he sabotaged my campaign.

"If you didn't want to help me, if you supported Marty as a candidate, then you should have had the decency to tell me at the start," I told him trying to keep my temper in check.

"It wasn't personal, Andrea. I like you and think you'd make a great president. Better than Marty Jenkins actually. It was pure economics. You offered me twenty dollars to help you and Marty offered me forty." He smiled.

His grin pushed me over the edge. He ruined my campaign—crippled my chance to get into Fitzpatrick All Girls Private High School, and then Harvard and then Yale—for twenty measly bucks. All of my rage came to a boil. I couldn't stop myself. I blew up. "You ruined my campaign over twenty dollars! Twenty stupid dollars!"

And then I grabbed the nearest thing and dumped it on his head—meatloaf!

Chapter Thirty-six

SUSPECT NUMBER THREE
☞ Joe Jacobs

I might have been okay, if it was one or the other. A flying ball of mashed potatoes or a plummeting brick of meatloaf. But it was both! Ralph and Andrea at the same time! Years of training at the Jacobs' table kicked in and there was nothing I could do to stop myself.

"FOOD FIGHT!" I yelled at the top of my lungs.

The Fight

A single ball of mashed potatoes, about the size of a softball, was flung across a crowded cafeteria. At the same time, a large slab of mangy meatloaf was being dumped on an unsuspecting Harold Wormald's head (although there is a chance he had an inkling of what was coming because several eyewitnesses claim he closed his eyes seconds before the slop was thrown on him.) The action didn't heat up until Joe Jacobs threw his own softball-sized mound of taters. Top athlete or not, he overshot his target and the potato ball sailed into a crowd landing with a *splat* in Rocks Mudman's bowl of soup. Soup wasn't on the menu that day but Rocks hadn't been feeling well the past few days and his mom sent him to school with a bowl of chicken noodle soup. The *splat* left Rocks covered in salty, lukewarm broth. It was then the fight really took flight.

Rocks grabbed a handful of Sludge Sludinksy's overcooked peas and carrots. Without a specific target in mind, he slung the food at the next table, leaving Genevieve Simon with a lap of mushy veggies. Furious that her new cashmere sweater was now green, orange and utterly ruined, Genevieve grabbed a slice of apple pie and vowed revenge. She knew the offending food had travelled from a north-west direction and that Ed Nojna was looking at her and snickering. Genevieve marched right over to Ed and smushed the pie in his face. Luckily for Ed the pie tasted pretty good for a cafeteria dessert. Only later did Genevieve find out that Ed was not laughing at her. Hannah Bennett had told him a very funny joke and Ed had a case of the giggles.

But, by then it was too late. Marlene Tang threw orange juice on Michael Wise as Adam Margols ducked for cover to avoid flying meat. Sarah Henley wasn't so fast on her feet and got a face full of peas. Hil Rotenberg tried to stay out of it, but slipped on a smear of potatoes as she tried to leave the cafeteria. And when Eldrick Hooperberg tried to help her up, he got pelted by another piece of pie—this one à la mode!

Snacks sailed through the air. Appetizers, main courses and desserts were all fair game. In less than three minutes, the J.R Wilcott cafeteria was coated in white, starchy potato sludge. Brown meatloaf stained the ceiling as smashed green peas covered kids and backpacks alike. Stringy, pulpy orange juice dripped from the tables while trampled apple pie left the floor carpeted in pale yellow.

Amid the chucks and dodges, Marty Jenkins stood with his eyes bulging in utter panic. During his usual self-imposed lunchtime competitive eating practice, he started choking on a meatball just as the fight began. Flailing his arms wildly, his sign for help went unnoticed among the slew of arms pitching food, until one Andrea Hackenpack raced toward his table and began the Heimlich maneuver. A few nearby students finally realized what was happening and watched as Andrea dislodged the meatball from Marty's mouth right into the back of Mr. Papernick's head. Just as the math teacher turned to see the source of the projectile, an impressively large heap of mashed potatoes splattered his front.

Soggy, mucky, utterly destroyed math tests lay limply in his hands. His fury cut through the chaos like a knife.

"STOP. RIGHT. NOW!" he bellowed thunderously, bringing an end to the madness.

Lock up

EPILOGUE
Andrea Hackenpack

Two weeks in detention. I had expected the punishment to be much worse.

"The way I see it Andrea," began Principal Losman, "you've been dealt a bigger punishment already."

He was talking about the election I lost. The final tally hadn't been close. I got trounced—taking barely ten percent of the vote. My dream of being J.R.Wilcott's next fearless leader and shaping the foreseeable future of the school was dead. But on the bright side, Marty Jenkins got trounced even worse. He only managed to pull two percent of the vote. Wilcotters, who evidently do not appreciate dirty politics, overwhelming chose Gwenn Yoon to be their next president. No one could recall what her platform had been, but it definitely didn't involve apps, advice or embarrassing your opponent. I wasn't sure what it all meant for my future plans but I had the next ten lunch periods to figure it out.

It took a whole afternoon in Principal Losman's office to sort out the big mess. Apps were opened and emails were retrieved—both sent and received—on everyone's phones before we could make total sense of the treachery.

"I love a good homophone as much as the next principal but this went too far," Principal Losman had said at the time. "Still, I have to give the three of you detention. According to the J.R. Wilcott student handbook, starting a school-wide food fight, with three different courses of food, is an offence you can be suspended over. Consider yourselves lucky with two weeks detention. I'll be having a chat with Mr. Jenkins later."

I was the first one to arrive and was eating my lunch when Ralph Dorph walked through the door. He smiled shyly and took a seat beside me.

"Ten days?" I asked him in a whisper. Mr. Kagan was busy marking papers and didn't seem to mind quiet chatter.

"Ten days," confirmed Ralph as he unpacked his lunch. It smelled delicious. I leaned over to get a better look and watched Ralph sprinkle salt and fresh lemon over his food.

"Edamame beans," he said noticing my interest. "I got hooked on them when I lived in Japan. Want to try some?"

I quickly gobbled a few and Ralph offered another handful. "They're delicious," I told him as I relaxed in my chair. "Did you live in Japan for a long time? What was school like there? Was there a Japanese version of that jerk, Marty Jenkins?"

Ralph smiled and leaned back in his chair. "There's a Marty Jenkins at every school. But only *this* Marty Jenkins is lunching with Principal Losman every Tuesday and Thursday for the next month, from what I heard."

"How did that happen?" I asked. "I thought you had a think tank with him on those days."

"I guess Principal Losman decided that I had enough on my plate with detention. And that it was more important to meet with Marty to discuss amending the student handbook campaign rules. I think there might be a page added that addresses sabotage."

Ralph handed me an extra pair of chopsticks before offering me a piece of vegetarian sushi. "What about Harold, though?" he asked. "He was the tech brains behind this whole thing and he got off scot-free. I mean, you lost the election over this, Andrea. Poor Joe has to live with poisoning Daniela. It doesn't seem fair that Harold's out there enjoying lunch."

"He might not have to spend extra time with Principal Losman or have to lunch in detention, but he got what was coming to him."

Ralph looked surprised so I explained. "You know the forty bucks that Harold made from Marty? He used it to buy a new video game for his 3DS, which was in his shirt pocket the whole time. It got completely ruined by meatloaf sauce! In the end, he got nothing for his plotting!"

"That's what I call getting your just desserts," laughed Ralph.

Suddenly, Joe Jacobs burst into the room like a tornado.

"Sorry, I'm late, Mr. Kagan! I had to let the chess guys know I'm not going to be with them for the next two weeks. They're gonna miss my moves," he grinned. "Hey, Mr. K., if you get bored these next two weeks, I'm down for a game of chess, checkers or Battleship. You name it."

Mr. Kagan couldn't help but smile. "You three keep it down in here. Remember this is supposed to be a punishment for inciting the largest food fight in J.R. Wilcott history—not to mention destroying Mr. Papernick's finest math test." He checked his clipboard. "From what I can see, it's just the three of you today. Take a few minutes and reflect on why you are here and how you can make better choices in the future." Classic teacher speak! "I want at least 100 words on the subject by the end of the period."

After a few minutes of writing I turned towards Joe, eager to take him up on his chess offer. But Joe was busy.

"It's great to finally get a chance to talk to you, buddy!

Losman's office doesn't count," he said to Ralph, grinning and holding up his hand for a high five. "I've been trying to hook up with you forever. Did I even thank you for the awesome tee? And find out how you write such killer rhymes? I definitely need your help there! I was thinking..."

Ralph looked surprised by Joe's enthusiasm and the fact that Joe's hand was way too high for Ralph to five. But Joe kept grinning and babbling and soon Ralph was also smiling.

I smiled and let out a big breath. "Ten days of this isn't so bad."

"Wait, why are you even here, Andrea?" asked Joe, confused. "How could Losman still give you detention after you saved Marty from that meatball?"

"I didn't tell him. None of the teachers saw me do it and there's no proof anyway. It's not like Marty's going to tell him."

"You saved Marty?" asked Ralph.

"All it took was a simple Heimlich. It's basic CPR."

"Made for a great action shot, too. Check it out." Glancing over at a distracted Mr. Kagan, Joe quietly took out his phone and showed me his screen. There was Marty, spewing out his meatball, and me, with my arms in the correct position beneath his ribcage, right behind him.

"Where did you get that?" I asked as Joe quickly slipped his phone back into his pocket.

"Everyone's been sending it to each other. Someone must've taken the photo while you were busy saving Jenkins. Someone probably sent it to you, too."

We snuck another look at Mr. Kagan who was still marking papers. The coast looked clear. I opened my phone, but before I could check my texts, I saw a red icon on the Bossypants app (™!). It said I had 124 unread messages!

"Whoa! Looks like your heroic gesture boosted your Bossypants following," said Ralph.

Ralph was right. If my math was accurate, over half of the school was following me now! My inbox was loaded with messages, like:

Dear Bossypants,

My best-friend asked out the boy she knows I like! I'm really mad at her and don't know what to do. Help!!!! For sure you'll know what to do in this situation.
Mad Bestie

Hey Andrea,

I want to go to a party next week and my parents won't let me. They don't trust me because last year I dressed up our dog in my mom's priceless pearl necklace and my dad's expensive watch. Then the dog jumped in the lake. The pearls and watch were never found again. How can I get them to trust me again?

Partyless Pal

And there was one particular message that stood out from the rest:

Hackenpack,

...thanks.

MJ

"Looks like your app is taking off," said Joe. "Oh, and there's more!" He took Andrea's phone and clicked a few times. "It's here somewhere," he said as he scrolled. "I think it's on the bulletin board you set up for people to post on."

Where can I sign up for Secret Lunch Menu Rounders?

Secret Lunch Menu Rounders sounds awesome. Can anyone join?

I have a secret way to throw soup. Sign me up for S.L.M.R's

The board was filled with Wilcotters asking about Secret Lunch Menu Rounders.

"But there's no such thing as Secret Lunch Menu Rounders," I reminded Joe. "You know this, Joe. It was just some dumb misunderstanding created by Harold's scheming."

"We've got something here, Andrea. Over 75 people asked about it! It's a longshot that the school would allow us to use leftover lunches, but we should be able to come up with something, even if it's not with meatloaf. We combine your brains, with my sports knowledge and Ralph's people skills and we'll have something awesome on our hands."

I was pretty sure Ralph agreed but I couldn't say for sure —I had already grabbed a pen and was making notes. *This* would be how I made my mark at school! Not many kids could boast they had a thriving advice app *and* a hand in creating a completely new sport! Fitzpatrick All Girls Private High School here I come... and then Harvard and Yale and perhaps even the Olympics!

"Do you think you could be my new tech manager for the app, Ralph?"

"Sure, I'd be happy to help."

"Great! And thanks for telling me about the photo, Joe. ... Joe?"

Joe was no longer paying attention to us. A new inmate had just joined us. Daniela Olafson handed a note to Mr. Kagan.

"Late to class?" Mr. Kagan looked surprised. "That doesn't sound like you, Daniela."

"Some things are worth being late for," said Daniela looking directly at Joe. Smiling, she took the chair beside Joe and offered him half of her bagel. Ralph and I exchanged knowing looks.

"So are you going to show Losman the photo?" asked Ralph.

I thought for a second. Maybe I could get my sentence withdrawn or at the very least reduced. But the more I thought about it, the less I wanted it to happen. "If Losman finds out, then I'll take whatever comes. But for now, you're stuck with me for a lunch mate."

Ralph smiled. "Happy to have you, Bossypants."